Jógvan Isaksen (born 1950) is a leading writer of contemporary Faroese crime fiction. This novel like many others features the dogged amateur detective Hannis Martinsson, who persists in his investigations when wiser counsel might often suggest a tactical retreat. The conflicts are played out against the wild and beautiful, but harsh and unforgiving backdrop of the Faroe Islands, a remote community used to relying on its own resources and solving its own dilemmas. Norvik Press has previously published the earlier novel *Walpurgis Tide* (*Krossmessa*, 2005). The recent TV drama series TROM was based on the Martinsson novels.

As well as writing detective fiction, Isaksen for many years taught Faroese language and literature at the University of Copenhagen, and is the prize-winning author of several books on Faroese literature and writers, among them William Heinesen and Jørgen-Franz Jacobsen.

Marita Thomsen is a literary translator and conference interpreter. Born in the Faroe Islands, she grew up in stories and between languages. She has made her way to Staffordshire via Peru and her retellings in English of Faroese literature include novels, poetry, plays and children's literature by authors such as Beinir Bergsson, Rakel Helmsdal, Sissal Kampmann, Marjun Syderbø Kjelnæs and Sólrún Michelsen. This is her first foray into crime fiction.

Some other books from Norvik Press

Jógvan Isaksen: *Walpurgis Tide* (Translated by John Keithsson)

Jørgen-Franz Jacobsen: *Barbara* (Translated by George Johnston)

Klaus Rifbjerg: *Terminal Innocence* (Translated by Paul Larkin)

Karin Boye: *Crisis* (Translated by Amanda Doxtater)

Fredrika Bremer: *The Colonel's Family* (Translated by Sarah Death)

Erik Fosnes Hansen: *Lobster Life* (Translated by Janet Garton)

Jan Kjærstad: *Berge* (Translated by Janet Garton)

Hagar Olsson: *Chitambo* (Translated by Sarah Death)

Ilmar Taska: *Pobeda 1946: A Car Called Victory* (Translated by Christopher Moseley)

Dan Turèll: *Murder in the Dark* (Translated by Mark Mussari)

For our complete back catalogue, please visit
www.norvikpress.com

DEAD MEN DANCING

by

Jógvan Isaksen

Translated from the Faroese
by Marita Thomsen

Foreword by Ivan Niclasen

Norvik Press
2023

Dead men dance on gritty sand
half-choked the baying knell
Grey seals barking close to land
An island in the night sun's spell

Christian Matras

Original title: *Deydningar dansa á sandi* © Jógvan Isaksen 2011.
Originally published by Mentunargrunnur Studentafelagsins, Tórshavn 2011.

This translation entitled *Dead Men Dancing* © Marita Thomsen 2023. The translator's moral right to be identified as the translator of the work has been asserted.

All poems in this volume are by Christian Matras. The poem on the title page is called 'Out in the Unbuilt' and was written in 1933, but was first published in *Á Hellu eg stóð* (On Bedrock I Stood), 1972. 'Dusk' was written in 1930 and published in *Heimur og heima* (World stage and homescape), 1933. 'Dark Memory' was published in the collection *Úr sjón og úr minni*, 1978 (also published in a bilingual edition, *Seeing and Remembering*, translated by George Johnston, Bloodaxe Books, 1986.)

Norvik Press Series B: English Translations of Scandinavian Literature, no. 86.

ISBN: 978-1-909408-72-2

Norvik Press
Department of Scandinavian Studies
University College London
Gower Street
London WC1E 6BT
United Kingdom
Website: www.norvikpress.com
E-mail address: norvik.press@ucl.ac.uk

Managing editors: Elettra Carbone, Sarah Death, Janet Garton, C. Claire Thomson, Essi Viitanen.

Layout and cover design: Essi Viitanen. Cover image Easton Mok for Unsplash.

FarLit

Norvik Press gratefully acknowledges the generous support of FarLit.

The Fatal Severing of Ties

For many, the Faroe Islands are a largely unknown archipelago far up in the North Atlantic. However, that image is gradually changing. Last year, viewers on Viaplay, BBC and Apple TV enjoyed the dark and thrilling series *Trom,* based on two of Jógvan Isaksen's crime novels about the Faroese journalist Hannis Martinsson. The internationally acclaimed Danish actor Ulrich Thomsen excelled in the role as the tight-lipped anti-hero, who is indignant at the mere thought that crime might actually pay.

With its bleak panoramas, the series sketched the contours of a small and tightly-knit community where tension or conflict could arise at almost any moment, whether they stemmed from decades of bad blood and enmity or were ignited by the fierce clash between old days and modern times. Such societies can certainly foster intriguing crime stories.

This spring, the picturesque islands once again formed the backdrop for a story with a classic touch, this time presenting themselves as the fabled Neverland in Disney's modernization of the story of Peter Pan and Wendy. The jagged mountain peaks, vertical lava cliffs and deep green valleys created a magical atmosphere, which resonated with the cinemagoers long after the lights were turned off. Another renowned character literally perished in the Faroe Islands. The steep island of Kalsoy formed the backdrop for the dramatic scenes in James Bond's last stand in the 2021 film *No Time to Die.* Today, 007's grave in the barren land is a favourite destination for the rapidly growing number of tourists coming to the islands.

However, it is not only the entertainment industry which has managed to make the Faroe Islands visible on the world map. The growing importance of the Arctic in the new geopolitical order has drawn the attention of the world to the societies in the high north. And if one focuses upon this small archipelago, which the well-known Faroese writer William Heinesen once compared to a grain of sand on the floor of a huge ballroom, the stark contrasts of a tiny yet hyper-modern community emerge.

The standard of living is amongst the highest in the western world. The newest underwater tunnel connecting two of the largest islands proudly presents the world's first roundabout under the seabed. And that's not all - the drive under the North Atlantic ocean floor offers a lavish light decoration and a huge iron sculpture of human-like figures encircling the roundabout. The internationally recognized artist Tróndur Patursson was inspired by the traditional Faroese chain dance, and thus tradition and modern construction go hand in hand deep under the sea. In the near future, a fourth underwater tunnel between the islands will open. It will be one of the longest in the world.

The Faroe Islands being an archipelago, it is only natural that a large part of its wealth is generated from the sea. The giant fishing trawlers are among the most modern in the world, and the fish-farming industry has, via investments and innovation, grown into a billion-dollar industry. The energy sector has come a long way with the green conversion to sustainable energy. As in other areas, there is a rapid development in modernizing society. This progress has provided fertile ground for an optimism and a drive which is not hampered by the fact that there are only 55,000 people living on the islands. In Germany, the host country for the upcoming European Championship finals in men's handball, people are still scratching their heads in disbelief that the

Faroe Islands managed to qualify – a feat that countries like Italy, Belgium and England failed to accomplish.

While the winds of change whirl over the islands, there are still strong and resistant bonds to the customs and values of traditional society. Where else in the world would you hear death notices being read out after the radio news? You cherish close family ties, and life and death are something you learn to share, not least when you have lived off the bounties of nature and with the whims of nature for centuries. No wonder that Christianity has a strong hold on the population, albeit mixed with a solid dose of fatalism.

It is in the gap between the new and the old that many of Isaksen's crime novels find their characteristic resonance. As a character, our hero Hannis Martinsson is another distant cousin of Philip Marlowe and Sam Spade and their descendants, who have sought justice in all sorts of large and small cities across most of the Western world. However, Isaksen's version of this classic anti-hero also manages to navigate between village and city, tradition and modernity, fate and Christianity. Martinsson is therefore more closely related to other North Atlantic investigators such as Jimmy Perez in Ann Cleeves' crime stories from Shetland and Erlendur Sveinsson in Arnaldur Indriðason's from Iceland.

A cruel murder marks the starting point for the action in *Deydningar dansa á sandi*. The key to the puzzle lies buried in a conflict which took place around seventy years ago in the second largest city, Klaksvík. The hostilities almost led to a state of civil war within the otherwise peaceful realm of Denmark. The well-liked Danish doctor in Klaksvík, Halvorsen, had a past in the Danish Nazi Party, and after a trial in 1953, he was denied the possibility of permanent employment. In the capital of Torshavn they wanted Halvorsen removed, and after a few years' deadlock, the dispute exploded with armed threats and the taking of hostages, armed Danish military and police in the streets and bomb blasts. The conflict, which was originally a rather banal matter, had evolved into something much more serious, resulting in a conglomeration of tensions between the capital and the periphery, Faroese separatists and unionists and the Danish military. But perhaps most tragically, the conflict tore the tightly-knit community of Klaksvík apart. To this day, all the wounds have not healed.

To Isaksen's credit, he has once again written an exciting crime novel which both provides an insight into Faroese history and paints a picture of Faroese society today.

Happy reading!

Ivan Niclasen
CEO, Faroese Broadcasting Corporation
August 2023

Sighing Eddies

Now night caresses the clover,
as the bluing hillside darkens.
Now hushed a night-wary whisper
swirls gently in sighing eddies.

1

He couldn't move. No matter how long or hard he pulled, his wrists were locked in. And his legs were just as stuck, it was as if his ankles were bolted to the rock. He'd been out cold, but was slowly regaining consciousness to find himself wedged between two boulders on the beach. He looked west towards the sleepy village of Leirvík and saw the headland Galvur on Kalsoy island gleaming in the morning sun. The sea was a little rough, he felt the surf wash over his paunch, and he was ice-cold below the belt.

What was this? Was it a dream?

The chill felt real enough.

He'd walked out along Kósin late last night to enjoy the sunset, but then something must have happened. He couldn't quite remember, it had gone dark all of a sudden.

He couldn't turn to check how high the sun hung in the sky, but estimated that it was probably about five in the morning. So he must have been out for nearly seven hours.

Little by little his head cleared, but he still couldn't comprehend any of this. Just knew that it was not some dream. This was real. Cruelly so. The sea was nearly at his navel now. His wrists were shackled in short iron chains bolted to rock; he could scarcely move.

How had he ended up here? And why was he shackled? He couldn't sit here soaked in the icy Atlantic. He called for help a few times, knowing full well that he was in the middle of nowhere and not a soul would be nearby at this hour.

A rising wind whipped up the waters and the tide was also gathering pace. Foaming breakers crashed against his chest; soon they would be rolling in over his head.

He realised that he would drown here. Someone had crafted this seat to drown people. To drown *him*. Terror rushed from his brain to rouse every cell in his body, but there was nothing to be done. He was well and truly tethered. Slowly it dawned on him that he *did* know why he was sitting here. He'd spent all his life running from this nightmare, and now he'd landed in its clutches.

The surf heaved across his face and his mouth filled with brine. He coughed and he spluttered, knowing at the same time that it would only get worse before it was all over.

2

A hefty black sack was hauled on board a boat that had approached the shore. Moments later the boat accelerated and sped northward. It was probably first bound for Klaksvík and then by road to the pathologist at the National Hospital in Tórshavn. The bag carried the body of a man, which the police had been notified of this morning. Rumour had it that the deceased had drowned, because he was chained between two boulders. He had been sitting there for days. Birds had feasted on his flesh, no doubt it had been a gruesome sight for the poor souls who found him.

A young police officer sat bent over on the grassy slope that framed the rocky foreshore. He'd helped to free the body, and I saw how he had to run off to vomit.

I was standing on a low crag watching the scene unfold below, while I pondered what the editor had told me. This morning at around ten he'd called me into his office and asked me to drive north to Klaksvík to find out what was going on there. A folk high school class from Tórshavn on an excursion to Fagralíð, the place where Føroya Fólkaháskúli was once located, had come across a body. The students were now receiving trauma counselling at Klaksvík Hospital and there wasn't a single shrink left in Tórshavn or its surroundings. They had all flocked north. The editor guffawed that this was quite the tasty little morsel for those quacks. And if they played their cards right they would be making hay until the end of the year.

Ten or so people were down at the foreshore. Two men were crouched at the tideline examining something. I was more than a hundred metres above, so I couldn't make out what they were looking at. Still, I assumed it to be the boulders the editor said the man had been shackled to.

Lord knows where he got the information. Then again, he had his sources everywhere, so there wasn't much this country could hide from him.

I'd intended to get closer to the crime scene, but had been ordered not to descend any further than this crag. Only people with business in the area were allowed closer. I played along.

A man and a woman were pacing the ruined grounds of the folk high school, and nearby three men stood huddled in conversation. Amongst them my old schoolmate Karl Olsen, leader of the Criminal Investigation Department in Tórshavn.

I could see Karl approaching the bloke who had emptied his guts; he put his hands on his shoulders and got him to his feet. Then they both trudged towards me.

I lit a cigarette and waited. Once they had made their ascent and were only a couple of metres away, I asked:

'Found anything, Karl?'

Karl halted and shot me a cold look. He was portly and his hairline was receding, but I knew that he wasn't to be trifled with. He opened his mouth a little, as if intending to reply, but then turned to the young officer.

'Come on, let's get back to the car.'

I stared at their backs as they walked away. Then I got angry. 'You could bloody well answer a normal question!'

Karl turned without stopping: 'I thought you'd quit smoking.' Then he marched on.

It hadn't always been like this between the two of us. In truth, it had *never* been like this between us, but we had fallen out.

For a moment I watched the people remaining below, and let my eyes drink in the beauty of this sunny day in early June. Leirvík was a picture of seaside idyll and there was not a trace of foreboding north in Kalsoy Fjord either. All sunlit mountains and white wisps of cloud drifting in a gentle breeze.

I ground the cigarette butt into the compacted gravel and followed the same path as my old friend.

On the road back to Tórshavn, I mulled over what had happened. Or, more precisely, what I knew about what had happened. And that, to be honest, was not much. Practically nothing at all. Still, it resonated with something at the back of my mind. I tried to tease it out, but it kept eluding me. So I switched on the radio to take my mind off it, then maybe later I would get on the right track. That sometimes worked.

The noon news bulletin was over and now they were reading out adverts about bingos and other events around the country. I listened with half an ear, but snapped to attention when the female news anchor, who was from Norðoyggjar judging from her dialect, said that they had just been told that a dead man had been found at Fagralíð, right below where the old folk high school was located a century ago. That was all they knew for now, but they would return to the incident in later newscasts.

I switched off the radio and tried again to figure out what was gnawing at the back of my mind. Had there been a forerunner to the man who drowned on the shore of Fagralíð? If so, who? It would not come to me, and I began to wonder whether I was misremembering or if I'd maybe just seen a film where someone suffered the same end. Still, I didn't think so.

Trapping a man between two rocks and leaving it up to the tide to do the rest was not everyday fare around these parts. And to my knowledge, not elsewhere either. But how exactly could it have come about?

Was it possible for one man to chain another to the foreshore? How had he managed to get him there in the first place? There was no road to Fagralíð, so unless someone had carried him nearly a kilometre, he must have walked there. Or been taken there by boat. However you looked at it, it was clear that this was no ordinary homicide. No doubt the murderer wanted the method to communicate something or other, and this was precisely what was rattling around my skull. It just kept slipping away from me.

Before leaving Klaksvík, I briefly considered seeking out the students and getting one of them to tell me their story. Though

I swiftly abandoned that possibility, both because it would be hard to get anywhere near the students at the hospital, and because they probably didn't have much to tell. Except for a horror story, of course, about a corpse in grisly condition, which had been the plaything of birds for several days. That story was not of much use to me anyway.

About half an hour later I parked the car on Skálatrøð overlooking the boats in the harbour and strolled towards the paper's office, Miðlahúsið. It was when I caught sight of the ravens on the statue of national hero, poet and smuggler Nólsoyar Páll that it came to me.

3

'Was Karl in good spirits?' the editor asked with a cynical smile. He was leaning back in his chair with his crossed legs resting on a corner of the desk.

'Not exactly,' I replied and took the seat opposite him.

'Thought as much,' the haggard dark-haired man scoffed and swung his legs off the desk. 'Did you find out anything?'

'Nah, not exactly, but I've an idea.'

'As everyone has an arsehole, so everyone has an idea.'

'*Opinion*!'

'Huh?' The editor looked puzzled.

'As everyone has an arsehole, so everyone has an *opinion*, not idea.'

'Whatever,' he made a sweeping hand gesture as if to brush my words aside. 'Right, so, you've had an idea.' There was a calendar on his desk, and he pulled it towards him. 'Please allow me to note this down.' He picked up a marker and mumbled as he wrote, 'Hannis had an idea.'

'Oh, bugger off!' I laughed. 'It's not *that* bloody exceptional that I come up with something.'

'Perhaps not, still, the occasion merits documenting.'

'Well, if you're capable of reining in the mockery for just a minute, then I'll tell you what came to my mind.'

'All right, go on then!' He leaned back in his chair again. 'But we have a paper to write, so summarise!' He nodded towards the big editorial room on the other side of the glass door. Staff were at their computers writing articles or working on layout, while two men and two women sat at the end of a long table discussing something. It seemed explosive, each face was redder than the last.

'Travel expenses,' the editor remarked.

'What?'

'I saw you looking at those four flushed faces. They're working on a series of articles about the Ministry of Foreign Affairs, and as we speak they're winding themselves up over travel expenses at said Ministry.'

'Ah, well, that's always been popular in this country. Both travelling and for anyone not invited along to fume about the expenses.'

'True, true,' the editor smirked. It would obviously take more than travel expenses to get him riled up. 'Now tell me about this idea of yours and get out, so I can work!'

'Up north in Fagralíð I couldn't get any closer to the body than watching from a crag overlooking the beach. But as I understood from what you told me, this was a bloke who was chained, and then abandoned for the sea to drown him at its leisure and for birds to peck at.' I glanced at the editor.

'According to my sources at the station, the deceased had been chained up there since Monday night at the very least. It's Thursday now, so you can imagine how he's been treated by the birds of the heavens over the last few days.' He huffed and shuddered.

'I'd rather not dwell on that,' I replied, 'but I think we've had a similar incident before.'

'I seriously doubt that,' the editor said and got up from his chair. 'This is so singularly brutal, I don't believe we've ever seen anything like it on our shores.'

It was obvious that he didn't want to believe what I was saying, but the fact that he'd abandoned his chair showed that I'd piqued his interest.

'You're familiar with Janus Djurhuus' poem about Nólsoyar Páll.'

'I don't know. Maybe. Spit it out, tell me what other incident of this nature has occurred in the Faroe Islands.' He paced over to the window and looked out.

I knew that he was looking straight down at the statue of Nólsoyar Páll with the ravens, but I took my sweet time. When you had the editor by the balls, there was no reason not to enjoy it!

'As I said, I didn't get much out of my excursion to Fagralíð, but on the way back to Tórshavn a hazy recollection occurred to me. It wasn't until I saw the statue of Nólsoyar Páll that it all came into focus.'

'Just bloody say it!' The editor looked peeved, and his sneering smile had evaporated.

'"Raven's caw over Beinisvørð, / cloud drift, night sun halved," and that's all I can recall.'

'And?'

'That was the opening line of Janus' poem about Nólsoyar Páll, which made me think of Mount Beinisvørð on Suðuroy, which in turn brought my memory to the surface. The keyword is *Beinisvørð*.'

'Beinisvørð!' The editor was still standing by the window and now he looked at me in astonishment. 'What on earth has Beinisvørð got to do with the murder in Fagralíð?'

I replied with another question. 'When was it that there was a rockslide on Beinisvørð?'

'Rockslide on Beinisvørð?' For a moment his face went entirely blank, then he pulled himself together. 'Are you all right, Hannis? I know that things haven't been great lately, but I had no idea that you were this close to the edge. If all those snake-oil sellers hadn't raced north to Klaksvík to tend to the folk high school students, I'd have suggested you go see one of them.'

'So you think me in need of a psychologist?'

'You know they don't rank high in my books, but I'm almost convinced you should go talk to one. I mean, I sent you north to Klaksvík to write about a dead man found chained in the fjord, and you come back here babbling about Nólsoyar Páll and Beinisvørð. Of course I don't think you're quite right in the head.' He studied me with concern.

I burst out laughing. 'To think I've lived to see the day. The editor of *Blaðið* displaying empathy for his staff. This must not get out under any circumstances, it would utterly ruin your reputation.'

'I don't go around worrying about my reputation,' the editor protested. 'It was you I was thinking of…'

'Oh shut it, will you,' I interrupted him. 'Just listen to me for a minute and forget about the counsellors. What Nólsoyar Páll and Beinisvørð got me thinking of was that thirty or forty years ago there was a rockslide on Beinisvørð. And it was no small one. Guillemot cliff ledges disappeared by the dozen, seal caves were closed off, and the entire profile of the headland changed. What I think I remember, and I don't know where I'm getting it from, is that when the dust settled the bones of a human arm were found on the shore unearthed by the rockslide.'

'I've never heard any of that, but so many a man has met his maker in those parts that it wouldn't be particularly odd if skeleton fragments were found.'

'With a shackle dangling from the wrist?' I asked, peering straight into the editor's dark eyes.

4

You could have heard a pin drop inside the office at Miðlahúsið. A distant drone of voices floated in from the editorial room and a lower-pitched humming came from the cars out in the street, but this office was like a tomb.

The editor was staring at me with his mouth half-open. His jaws were moving as if he wanted to say something, but couldn't get a word out. Then he reached for his calendar and looked down at it.

'There's no need to commit this to paper,' I said. 'First I have to find out what happened there a lifetime ago.'

'I have no intention of writing down what you told me, I was checking the date. Making sure it wasn't April fool's.' The editor gave me a searching look.

'I'm telling the truth. The trouble is that I can't for the life of me remember where I heard it.'

'How come you supposedly heard of this shackled arm, when I haven't heard a whisper?'

'I don't know, but I'm absolutely certain it was shared with me years and years ago. Somebody told me the story shortly after the event, but I clearly only took notice of this thing about the shackle. So I can't even recall who did the telling.'

The editor didn't exactly look convinced when he rumbled: 'You get sent to Fagralíð to dig up something new on the deceased found chained on the foreshore. You can't get near the body, you're not on particularly good terms with the police. Instead you come here telling me that you had a dream about the bones of some shackled arm found at the foot of Beinisvørð.'

'I didn't dream it…'

The editor cut me off: 'You might as well have dreamt it all since you haven't the foggiest where you got that story from.'

I shut up.

The editor tapped his keyboard and then said, 'According to Wikipedia there were rockslides on Beinisvørð in both 1975 and 1976, and these were major ones. So you're right on that count, but there's no mention here of any skeleton or arm sup-posedly found.' He turned to me. 'Why would you bring me a not even half-digested story? Why didn't you wait until you found something tangible?'

'Well, that was my first intention, but on my way in here I walked past Nólsoyar Páll and that's when the penny dropped. I spent the entire drive from Klaksvík trying to dig out of my head what the dead person in Fagralíð reminded me of. I sup-pose you just had the misfortune of crossing my path right as I figured out what I'd been racking my brain to find all the way south.'

' *"For of the abundance of the heart his mouth speaketh,"* ' the editor quipped, and I could see the glint in his eye.

'Something like that. It wasn't my intention to bother you with this. At least not yet. On the other hand, I would very much like to be given leave of absence for two weeks.'

'Two weeks? We're understaffed as is and we plan to make a big splash of the gruesome goings-on up north.'

'I know, but I'm convinced I can track down a much bigger story.'

'Don't you think you're blowing this out of proportion? We have a singularly macabre murder, and you think that you can recall something from the mid-1970s, are you planning on link-ing these two events?'

'Bingo! And for that I need time.'

'Hannis, my friend, we know there was a rockslide on Bein-isvørð, but you're the only one who knows that a shackled arm was found. We're in the business of writing and publishing a paper, not tales of there being more things between heaven and earth than ordinary folk suspect.'

'Hey, easy on the sarcasm,' I replied. 'All I'm asking for is two weeks, and if nothing comes of it, you won't have to pay me for them.'

The editor sighed; 'You know full well that you're grasping at bloody straws, but you'll be the one paying for it.'

He stared into space for a moment, 'All right, you have two weeks and not a day longer. Now get out, so I can call our managing director Kim Hentze and tell him that he'll have to come in. You know he's been on leave for almost two years writing about the airport affair, but now that you'll be off chasing ghosts, he'll have to come to work for a few days. The airport certainly won't be going anywhere,' the editor concluded with a chortle.

'The body from Fagralíð will hardly be going on any long walks either. Those days are probably over,' I said and headed out the door.

On my way down the stairs I mused that there wasn't much rhyme or reason to my parting statement. As to whether there was any to the whole foregoing conversation with the editor, well, time would tell.

5

The weather was nice enough that I decided to stroll along the waterfront to the National Hospital. Had it been a few months ago, I would have stopped by the station to ask the police what they'd found in connection with the rockslide in Beinisvørð. But I'd gone from regular to *persona non grata* down at the station. My girl, my partner Duruta, was an officer and we had an almost thirteen-year-old daughter together. We'd each lived in a terraced house all these years, she in East Tórshavn and I out West. It all worked quite well for us, though Duruta regularly nagged that I drank too much and didn't take sufficient responsibility for our daughter, Turið. I didn't think the latter was true, though there may have been something in the former, but most of my friends enjoyed a drink. And so did I. On the other hand, I'd always done my job, and the bottle had never come between me and anything I'd committed to. So I didn't consider myself a drunkard, but clearly there were others who did.

Even so, that wasn't the issue. Last summer Duruta moved to Denmark to take a course at the Police Academy, because she wanted a transfer to the Criminal Investigation Department, and she took our daughter with her. I did offer to have Turið come live with me while Duruta was in Denmark, but she hadn't even bothered with a reply to that. While Duruta was away, I carried on writing for *Blaðið*, but unlike the old days when I was freelance, I now had a permanent position. This meant that I got invited to staff functions, and at one of those parties I crossed the line. I'd invited a nurse as my plus one to the Christmas party, and afterwards we ended up at home in my bed. The nurse and I were about the same age and she had grown children, so we weren't thoughtless teenagers. When she went home around noon the next day, she told me there was something she was missing, something she couldn't find. I only listened with half an ear and didn't take much note. My head was heavy and I was sleep-deprived too.

The following day I tidied up as best I could and changed the sheets, because Duruta and Turið were coming home for Christmas and would be staying with me. Duruta had let her house for the year she would be away.

There was great joy and excitement when I welcomed them at the bus terminal. I hadn't seen them since the autumn break, and Turið seemed much more adult than last time and Duruta more beautiful than ever. When we got to my place Turið went straight out to visit a friend, promising she would be back for dinner in about two hours. Duruta and I wound up in bed, but shortly after she came out of the bathroom holding a pair of black panties. She said she'd found them behind the toilet. There wasn't much I could do other than own up and tell her the truth, that I'd spent the night with a woman after the office Christmas do.

Duruta didn't say a word. Got dressed, grabbed her and Turið's luggage and walked out. I tried pleading with her, but to no avail. She didn't deign to answer. Shortly afterwards Katrin, Karl's wife, swung up in their car and left with Duruta.

There I stood, no partner, no daughter, and my old friend Karl, who I tried to contact, also refused to talk to me. There was nothing I could do, and soon after New Year Duruta went back to Denmark with my daughter. The day before they left, Turið came to visit and she scolded me: how could I be so stupid as to run after other women when I had her mum? When she left she still gave me a hug, though, and a peck on the cheek, and told me to try and behave in future.

This, in a nutshell, was why I'd fallen out with much of the police force. It seemed like everyone was on Duruta's side and no-one was on mine. But that isn't the end of the story. In the spring I heard that Duruta was pregnant and was due in August. I called her to ask who the father was. She replied that she couldn't see how that had anything to do with me, but that she could assure me that it definitely wasn't mine. She'd found someone else when she returned to Denmark, and he was the father of the child, and it was none of my sodding business who she was with. It was the last time I'd spoken to Duruta.

The saying goes that no one is fully mocked until he mocks himself. That's precisely how I felt. I felt fully mocked, but was trying to live with it. The beautiful nurse had called me and asked if we should meet again. I ummed and aahed until she sensed that something was the matter, and then just said goodbye and hung up. My only comfort these last months had been that Turið phoned me regularly to chat about this and that, but she never breathed a word about what her mum was up to. Just talked about herself, school friends and life in Copenhagen, which she really enjoyed.

It was nearing three in the afternoon when I passed the ship wharf, and after I crossed the road down to the quay, I stopped to take in the fjord. The silvery sea was dotted with little boats. The scene brought Haraldur to mind. He would no doubt have been out fishing on a day like today, and if things had been different, I might have been out there with him. The thing was that Haraldur had married his girlfriend Sanna, and they took off travelling a whole month ago, vowing not to return until it was time for the autumn sheep drives. They were well and truly grownup, older than me, childless, so why not just find some beach to laze on for a few months. Haraldur had always been a rock, and now that he was away, it made my lot that much lonelier.

I set off again, thinking that in reality I only had one close friend left in this country, and he was out at the hospital. Edmund West was a history professor at the University of the Faroe Islands, and I visited him regularly. He was always friendly and welcoming and ready with good advice. We also had a shared interest in Scottish single malt whisky. But just under a week ago he'd been hospitalised, because his kidneys weren't functioning as they should, and he was running a high fever.

When I visited him, he'd been in good spirits and insisted that this was just some minor bother, which the quacks at the hospital would sort out in no time. As I left I enquired about his prognosis with one of the doctors, and he'd been less confident than the patient, but said that he couldn't say anything for certain.

The hospital had been considerably expanded in recent years, but it still wasn't hard to find the inpatient medical ward where Edmund was. The patient seemed to be in a good mood and beamed a bearded smile at me as I entered the suite.

'Here comes the cavalry!' Edmund boomed so loud that it echoed down the corridor. 'Nurse! Bring the glasses, it's whisky o'clock.'

'Not on yer life!' said a voice in a Suðuroy singsong behind me. 'Not a drop of booze will wet yer lips as long as ye're in this bed.'

She was smiling, red-haired and freckled. And beautiful too, as most young women are before childbirth and pig-headed men leave their mark. She eyed me.

'I hope ye havnae brought any drink for that clown. His kidneys cannae take it, and we'd like to keep him here with us a few more years.' She went back out to the corridor and closed the door behind her.

'Her mum and I are second cousins,' Edmund smiled. 'An attractive woman. Well, that applies to both mother and daughter,' he added.

'How goes?' I asked.

'Aye, all is well, very well indeed.' He was clearly in a buoyant mood.

'Well, aren't you enjoying yourself.'

'Why, is there any reason not to?'

'No, perhaps not, but I remember my great-grandma saying that it takes good health to be in hospital. And here you lie looking as if you've never been better.'

'I wouldn't say that. I miss my cheroots, but smoking is banned at the hospital, so there's nothing for it. Other than that, being here isn't too bad. The food is decent and it's crammed with pretty young women.'

'Getting better?'

'They don't know anything yet. They're doing so many blood tests that I'm like a pincushion. But they've managed to bring down the fever from over 40 to below 39.'

The room had south-east-facing windows, and I went over to have a look. The view was certainly nice.

'Ye just visited the day before yesterday. How come ye're already back to see me again?'

Edmund looked searchingly at me. I approached his bed and pulled up a stool.

'They found a body north in Fagralíð.'

'I know, I heard it on the radio, but they just said that a man had been found in the fjord. What was it about this man that brings you here?'

'The radio didn't say that the man was shackled to a boulder on the foreshore. Chained so that he'd drown at high tide.'

'I'll be damned,' Edmund huffed. 'I've never heard of anything like that here in the Faroes before. Or anywhere else for that matter.'

'Well, it's certainly out of the ordinary. The killer put in a lot of effort to make sure that his prey would die in exactly this manner.'

'Ye mean like he's trying to communicate something. Send a message?'

'Yeah.'

'But what's the message, apart from the sheer torture of sitting on the foreshore waiting to slowly drown.' Edmund looked pensive.

'No clue, and I don't know who the deceased is either.'

Edmund smirked, 'I imagine that yerself and the police station are not precisely on the good old terms ye used to be.'

'No, but we'll figure out who the victim is. I'm fairly certain the editor already knows by now.'

'Aye, that devil has ears everywhere,' Edmund replied. 'But, hey, aren't the two of ye related?' He shot me a teasing look.

'Look, I'm third cousins with at least half of the Faroes, so it's hard to find anyone I'm *not* related to. But never mind all that,' I continued. 'The reason why I came to see you is because someone has been chained on the foreshore before.'

'What?' The smile evaporated from Edmund's face, and he looked at me with a serious expression now. 'Are ye saying that another person has been killed so brutally in these isles before?'

'Aha, I think so.'

'Really?' Edmund looked very doubtful.

'Yes.'

It was quiet for a moment, and we could hear the clatter and footsteps from the hall.

'I don't usually question yer conjectures. Though the gods know they're often far-fetched, more often than not yer theories prove correct. But this time I do think ye're wading out pretty deep.'

'Perhaps, but not so far that I haven't got my head above water.'

'Fine, but ye'll have to tell me what ye've got hold of. I certainly haven't heard of anything like this in all ma days.'

'Right, well, then I came here in vain. I'd pinned my hopes on you.'

'Some hope. I'm lying here on a hospital ward, bedridden like Ole Morske in his loft in that old ballad. But, do tell!'

So I told Edmund how the shackled man had got me thinking about the bones of an arm with a chain and iron shackle, which had been found at the foot of Beinisvørð after a rockslide.

'I was studying in Denmark at the time,' Edmund said. 'If I'm not mistaken it was in 1975 and 1976, and the good folk of Sumba village lost a chunk of their pride. But how come this never came out?'

'I don't know, and it's also a problem that I can't remember who told me about the arm.'

'Aye, well, that doesn't make the picture any clearer. And the connection is tenuous as is.'

'True, but there's something to this. I know there is,' I insisted, and carried on: 'And then, well, I remembered that you're from Vágur, just the next village over. You can't get much closer to Beinisvørð, unless you're actually from Sumba.'

'All right, all right, I'll play along,' Edmund smiled, 'and I think I have the name of the person who would know all about this. Assuming there's something to know, that is,' he added.

6

It had gone four by the time I strolled home along Hospitals-vegurin, and I was trying for the umpteenth time to rack my brains. Someone, years ago, had told me about an arm found at the foot of Beinisvørð. And that it had an iron shackle with the stump of a chain around its wrist. This precise image was etched into my mind, but no matter how I approached it, I could not for the life of me remember who told me the story. Sooner or later it would come to me though.

That Edmund knew nothing about the arm bones almost made me wonder if I was misremembering. Almost. Though Edmund West in my eyes was practically omniscient, there was only one who knew everything – according to the Bible, of course – and his name wasn't Edmund.

Then again, Edmund had promised to call his father's cousin who'd been a police officer south on Suðuroy at the time. He was approaching ninety, but with a mind as clear as Aalborg Red aquavit, he'd added with a chuckle. Just then a doctor came in to do the rounds. She was a Danish consultant, who said her name was Karen Vejen and asked me to leave. She was blonde and stunning, and though she must have been over sixty, she was in good shape.

Over the wall of people who shortly after encircled his bed, Edmund shouted that I could come back tonight, by then he would have spoken to the old officer about that arm with the iron shackle.

Leaving the ward I hoped that what Edmund had meant by his words was that the old man was as clear as the drink, and not that he was as muddled as the rest of us get when we indulge in too much of it.

My yellow and red duplex was at the far end of Jóannes Paturssonargøta. I'd never been terribly fond of it, it was poorly insulated and could hardly be entered for any architectural prize. Still, it had three decent-sized floors and that was more than enough for me. The house sat right on the pavement and close to the neighbouring house, but behind it there was a garden, of sorts. I didn't exactly grow up in an orchard, so the ground was mostly compacted dirt with some gravel thrown in.

I headed up the stairs to the first floor, where the kitchen and living room were. The top floor had three snug rooms and a bathroom. The basement I'd never really done much with, so it was mostly filled with junk, and days would go by between my trips down there.

I was thirsty for a drink or a whisky, but dropped that plan. I wasn't in a particularly good mood, and hadn't been for a long time, and times like these I tried to stay clear of the strong stuff. I had several acquaintances who looked to the bottle for support through rough patches, but in those situations it always proved a faithless friend.

So I sat down at the kitchen table instead, lit up a cigarette and tried to let my mind wander. It was no use. My thoughts kept circling back to my family, and I had visions of Duruta and Turið. Tried to brush them aside, but they resisted. It wasn't that I was jealous, didn't think I had any right to be, but still. Anyone can stumble, and I had, big time. My punishment was that Duruta had left me, and was now expecting a baby with another man. But the worst of it was going so long between seeing Turið. Then again, Turið would be a teenager soon, and by that point you have no control over them anyway.

This wasn't getting me anywhere. I stubbed out the cigarette, went upstairs and lay down in bed. Maybe a short nap would clear my mind.

My head was heavy and I was cruising towards slumber land. In that split-second, halfway between waking and dreaming, what I'd been trying to dredge up came to me, and I was wide awake. While I lay staring at the ceiling, I pictured a big room with a heaving crowd. On the floor, backs against the wall, Karl and I were sitting, each holding a beer. We were at some party. We were very young, and I thought I remembered that Karl, who was studying at the Police Academy, had just returned from a work placement back in the Faroes. I had a hazy recollection that some left-leaning political organisation had organised the gathering, and that I'd dragged Karl, my old schoolmate, along, though he wasn't much into hanging out with lefties. A couple of beers and schnapps had helped him come to terms with *The Internationale* being belted out, but soon the revellers turned to satirical panto songs such as 'Eg eri bert ein miðal hampamaður' and 'Sektus og sekterius'. If I was not mistaken, the party was taking place at the Faroese Association's Copenhagen stronghold, Føroyahøli, in Rantzaugade, and, as regards the fairer sex, neither Karl nor I would go home without a catch.

Sitting there on the floor, Karl told me that he'd spent a few weeks on Suðuroy working at the police station in Tvøroyri, and that he and another officer had visited Sumba. There had been a rockslide on Beinisvørð a few days earlier, and when boats had approached the debris, they'd found bones. They'd brought them back to Sumba and called the police.

The policemen immediately realised that something was amiss. It was one thing to come across the remains of a skeleton, but a shackled wrist with a chain was an ominous portent. They asked locals to sail them to the foot of Beinisvørð and show them where they'd found the arm. The rockslide was colossal and there was widespread shattered detritus, but they couldn't spot any further remains of any skeleton from the boat. There was no sending a search party either, both because of the very slim prospects of finding anything, and because of the continued danger of crushing boulders raining down.

Karl had returned to Denmark soon after, and that night at the party he told me about this incident. I had more than a few drinks on board when I got the story from Karl, but the image of the shackles on what had been a man's arm had etched it-self into my mind. I doubted that I'd spared the arm a thought in the three decades since, but the image had still been there deep in my unconscious.

It was, of course, by no means certain that the dead man in Fagralíð and the one they had found an arm of in the mid-1970s were linked in any way. And yet both had been chained, so I intended to find out if there was a connection.

7

It was nearing dinnertime when I left my car at the seafront on Yviri við Strond. The old station in Jónas Broncksgøta Street had turned out to be mould-infested, so now the police force was based at rented premises across from the Eik Bank head office.

As I got out of the car I noticed an odd quiet. There were no cars out front and not a soul in sight.

The reception was staffed by a lone young woman, who told me that she was guarding the fort, as most of the crew was up in Norðoyggjar. However, Karl was also at the station, and I would locate him if I headed up to the third floor and then continued all the way down to my right. I had the impression that a smile lurked in the corner of her eye and I had no doubt that this woman, who was a stranger to me, knew all about me and Duruta. Those were the conditions in this country. If you wanted to live in a society where the number of inhabitants wasn't huge, and folk therefore took an interest in each other, then you had to accept the flipside, that they knew practically everything about you. And talked about it. It was probably part of the explanation why half of the Faroese who moved abroad to study never moved back home again. They'd become used to being just one more in a crowd and could no longer cope with the alternative.

Karl's office was south-facing with a full panorama of the fjord. A considerably prettier view than the narrow Bókbinda-ragøta streetscape he could see from his previous windows.

He was seated at a desk with his back turned to the splendour outside, and his expression when he spotted me was not exactly welcoming. He didn't utter a word, though, just fixed me with a piercing scowl.

I was expecting this, so I jumped straight in. 'Aeons ago at a party in Copenhagen, you told me about the remains of an arm which had been found at the foot of Beinisvørð, and that there was a shackle around its wrist, as though its owner had been chained.'

Karl seemed taken aback, and looked as though he was debating whether to lay into me, which he clearly had an urge to do, or whether he should pursue the subject of the arm.

I watched the inner struggle play out, until the policeman, the detective, won out. I still got snapped at: 'You've got some nerve showing up here, when you know full well what I think of you and how you've treated Duruta.' For a moment he glared straight into my eyes. 'But we'll leave that aside. For now.' He leaned back in his chair with an appearance bordering on normal, and said:

'So you remembered what I told you back then.' A smirk hid at the corners of his mouth. 'It occurred to me as soon as I saw you in Fagralíð that a bastard like you would probably remember that story.'

'You hadn't forgotten that you told me about that arm?'

'No, I hadn't. Strange thing is, though, that I've hardly thought about it since, and I haven't heard a word about it either. That may all change now.'

'You're saying *may all change*?' I blurted out and found a chair. 'There's hardly any *may* about it.'

Karl broke into a broad smile, and it did me good, because I hadn't seen it in months. 'Spoken like a true hack looking for a titillating story. See, that's not how the police operates.'

'What kind of drivel is that?' I was getting a little worked up. 'In 1975 the arm of a skeleton is found at the foot of Beinisvørð after a rockslide. Around the wrist there's a shackle with the stub of a chain. And this morning a man is found drowned on the Fagralíð foreshore, and he's chained to a couple of boulders. This kind of murder doesn't happen every day, not here or anywhere else, so what are you waiting for?'

'Hey, calm down,' Karl raised a hand in a soothing gesture. 'You're getting ahead of yourself linking *A* and *Ø* without even considering all the letters in between.'

'This is no alphabet, this is murder, maybe several murders!' I half shouted.

'If you don't take it down a notch, I won't bother talking to you at all,' Karl said with determination.

I shut my trap, realising that I might have gone in too hard. Somehow I'd been feeling under so much pressure for a while now that I didn't always have a grip on myself. 'Fine,' I said eventually, 'but there has to be a sodding connection.'

'Why?' Karl watched me with an innocent gaze.

'It's obvious. The shackles around the wrists!'

'You're making that classical amateur mistake. You've got a piece of information, which might be reminiscent of another, and you immediately insist there's a connection. That the two are somehow related.'

'I'm fully aware that it's been thirty-odd years since that arm was found down south, and that it was only today that a bloke was found chained to the shore. But the possibility of a connection at least needs looking into.'

'Of course it needs looking into, but it isn't that easy.'

'Why?'

'Plenty of reasons. First of all we have our hands full with the drowned man in Fagralíð. Bergur Mjóvanes is in charge up north and I'm sitting here trying to coordinate everything. We've only just managed to find out who he is. The body was in terrible condition, what with the birds and sitting in the surf for days.'

'Who was he?'

'We had a hell of a time trying to suss that out. We took pictures of him and got someone here to patch him up in Photoshop, so he wouldn't look quite as nightmarish. Then we went from door to door in Klaksvík, but for ages nobody had a clue who he was. It wasn't until we tried at a care home that we managed to identify him. There, several people knew him. The name is Ísak Joensen, and he spent most of his life in Iceland.

This was his first visit back since he moved abroad in the mid-fifties.'

'And then he gets killed.'

'Indeed he does, even though he's only been back two days. Retracing old paths is clearly a risky business.'

'Was he running away from anything when he moved?'

'We don't know. Not yet at least. For now, we've just identified who he is, that he was from Klaksvík, and that he was staying at the sailors' lodgings Sjómansheimi while he was here.'

'Surely that doesn't stop you linking him to the chained arm from Beinisvørð.'

'No, it doesn't. But there's one more thing.'

'What?'

'The arm is gone.'

8

'Gone?' I said, stunned. 'How can an arm just go missing?'

'I'm as puzzled as you are.' Karl rose, turned his back to me and gazed out the window as he went on: 'I don't know how much I told you about the shackled arm at that communist piss-up.'

'It wasn't any communist piss-up...' I tried to protest, but Karl cut me off.

'Sod the damn party! I don't bloody care what the Marx-ist-Leninists of Oyggjaframi and the Maoists were squabbling over in Copenhagen forty years ago.' He shrugged emphati-cally. 'How much did I tell you?'

For a moment I fully intended to argue the cause of the left-ies in Copenhagen, but my better angels rallied and I replied: 'You told me that the bones of an arm had been found after the Beinisvørð landslide. That there was an iron shackle around the arm, that's why the Tvøroyri police was sent for, and that you went out to Beinisvørð to take a look. I don't think you said any more than that.'

'Well, that's also very nearly all I knew then.' Karl stood in silence for a moment, then muttered, to no one in particular: 'The view from here truly is spectacular. You won't find any bet-ter in these parts. I wouldn't mind getting to stay here.'

'The arm, Karl.'

'Huh?' It was as if he woke from a slumber. 'Ah, yes, the arm. Kalurin and I...' He paused. 'They called the other officer Kal-urin, and I can't for the life of me remember his Christian name. South on Suðuroy everyone had a moniker, and not a devil knew what their real names were. Never mind. Kalurin and I went to Sumba to perform a post-mortem on the arm. We expected to find it down at the landing, but nobody was there. Up in the village we were told that they'd taken the arm to the church, they didn't really know what else to do with it.

'In the church we found the arm on the altar. We looked at it and noticed that they'd tried to piece it together, bone by bone, and they'd done a pretty good job of it too.'

Karl stopped, as though he was pondering something, then resumed, 'It was a left arm and around the wrist there was a shackle and from it dangled a couple of rusty chain links. We wrapped the arm in a canvas bag we'd brought along, and left it in the boot of the car. Then we went looking for the people who found the arm. Turned out to be three blokes from the same house, a father and two grown sons, who told us that they'd left the arm in the church on account that maybe it belonged to a Christian. They also said that, in spite of the rockslide, the way they found the bones lying left no doubt that it was a human arm with a hand and everything.'

Karl turned back towards me. 'You could spend hours just taking in a view like this. Probably just as well that we're moving back up to Jonas Broncksgøta, so that we can get some work done.' He sat back down in his chair.

'We had the father and sons sail us west to the foot of Beinisvørð, it only took a good half hour. The rockslide was tremendous, the cliff had a whole new outline, but the Sumba men showed us where they found the arm. We could see straight away that it was impossible to go searching for the rest of the skeleton, and it wasn't possible to guess from which part of the cliff it had come.'

'So it could just as well have come from above as below?' I asked.

'From above, yes, perhaps, but I don't get what you mean by below?'

'I'm thinking of the caves, the seal caves. Believe I heard somewhere that there were several seal caves below Beinisvørð, and that many of them were decimated when the cliff face came crashing down.'

'Aha, the locals did talk about that. In addition to dead birds, they'd also found some dead seals. But what does that have to do with the arm?'

'The man in Fagralíð was chained to the foreshore and he sat there for several days, because people don't go there very often. If a man was ever chained on the foreshore below Beinisvørð, then the good folk of Sumba would have spotted him on their fishing trips.'

I looked at Karl, who nodded his agreement.

'But if a man was chained inside one of the caves, then they wouldn't have seen him.'

'They've been harvesting seals for centuries, and they would have come across him on a hunt.'

'I doubt that they've hunted any seals since World War II, so he could have been sitting there for a long time.'

'Perhaps, but not for as long as we calculated on that day in Sumba in 1975.'

'What do you mean?'

'When we got back to the village, the finders invited us to dinner and offered beer and schnapps to chase it down. As the evening went by, more and more people dropped in, and it half turned into a party. There was a lot of speculation about where that arm might have come from, but there was one thing the gathering agreed on, and that was that it didn't come from any Faroeman. So talk soon turned to the *Westerbeek*, which ran aground south of Lopranseiði.'

'I've heard of the *Westerbeek* shipwreck out by those bird cliffs, but what does it have to do with this?'

'According to the people of Sumba, quite a lot,' Karl replied and glanced at his watch. 'Have you had dinner?'

'No.'

'Well, Katrin is with her knit and natter tonight, so there's no dinner on the cards. How about the two of us go find a place where we can get a bite?'

He could see that I was staring at him. It felt to me like a very sudden change had come over Karl. From not deigning to reply to me this morning, to suggesting that we have dinner together.

'You look puzzled, but I haven't been too happy either that this thing with you and Duruta has kept us from seeing each other. I mean, we go way back.'

'I think so too, but why have you been so skittish, to use a nice word, all these months?'

'It's Katrin. She's bloody furious that you cheated on her friend.' He chuckled to himself. 'Not long ago I overheard her on the phone with Duruta, and it rather sounded as if Duruta was trying to smooth the waters on your behalf.'

Karl got up and put on a jacket, which had been hanging behind the door.

'Come on, let's go find a place to eat. I don't have that long, I've got to get back here to try to keep on top of anything that comes in. It'll probably take most of the night.'

'How about...?'

'I'll tell you the rest of the story over dinner,' Karl interjected.

We went to Hotel Hafnia, where they had steamed haddock on the menu. We asked for a lager each to go with it.

While we waited for dinner and then ate it, Karl told me about that night in Sumba many moons ago.

'They claimed that the arm likely came off one of the *Westerbeek* crew. The ship was a Dutch East India Company vessel. On its way home from Ceylon, it veered off course in dense fog and the upshot was that the ship got smashed to smithereens and sank not far north of Beinisvørð. Nearly all the crew were saved, because they managed to climb up the mast and then walk along a yardarm to reach a large bird ledge on the cliff.'

'When was this?'

'If memory serves, it was 1742 and in September, I think.' Karl had a drink of his beer.

'I'm guessing,' I said, 'that the locals insisted that the bones they'd found were from one of the ship's crew.'

'Precisely, and they also claimed that something supernatural was at play.'

'Supernatural?'

'Mm, because how come an arm, with no tendons, cartilage or flesh left on it, can lie in a rockslide in the exact shape of a real arm.'

'No clue. But I'd have my doubts about there being anything ghostly at play.'

'Rightly so,' Karl laughed, 'but don't tell anyone from Sumba. At least not when you're sharing a drink with them. It could well cost you your life, they're strong as trolls. Their conclusion was that this was the arm of someone who'd been chained on board when the ship was lost, and who now had resurfaced. That the bones were laid out in that way, was a sign that we should beware of some looming peril.'

'The chained arm was a warning.'

'That's what the folk of Sumba said that night, which turned out to be a great one with lots of stories and a fair few chanted ballads.'

'What, pray, were we meant to beware of?'

'They didn't have any opinion on that, but mused that so much was hidden from human eyes. "The Lord giveth and the Lord taketh away; blessed be the name of the Lord," was their conclusion.'

'I understand full well why people used to be so fond of the *Book of Job* in this archipelago, where so many people died elsewhere than in their bed, but what happened to the arm?'

Karl ate the rest of his haddock, shunted what was left of the sides onto a fork and said, before stuffing it into his mouth, 'That's precisely the question.'

I waited impatiently to hear more, but had sufficient wits about me to wait until Karl had finished eating.

'The next morning, well, it was nearing noon, when we'd driven back north to Tvøroyri, we discussed the arm and agreed that the people of Sumba were probably onto something. Not about the superstition, but that the arm probably belonged to someone on the *Westerbeek*, and that the rockslide had brought it out from where it had been lying for over two hundred years.'

A waiter approached to clear our plates, and we complimented the chef on the haddock and ordered coffee. When the waiter had left, Karl continued: 'Only a few days later I went to Tórshavn and then back to Denmark to the Police Academy, and I just presumed that someone would take care of the arm. Bury it in a cemetery or something. I mean, it's happened several times in the Faroes, including here in Tórshavn, that ancient long-forgotten burial sites have re-emerged. And people have just gathered up the bones, stuffed them in a coffin or barrel and reburied them.'

'At the station you said that the arm was gone.'

'So it is. Shortly after I returned to Denmark, Kalurin called me to ask if I knew where the arm had gone to. I told him the truth, that the last I saw of it was when we put it in the car boot. But it wasn't there any more, and Kalurin swore that he hadn't taken it. We agreed that it was no tragedy: if it had endured lying at the bottom of the sea for centuries, then it could probably also stand going missing in Tvøroyri for a bit.'

Coffee was brought to the table, and the waiter poured us two cups.

'That's the last I know of the shackled arm found by Sumba men.' Karl sipped his coffee and continued: 'Until today, I've barely spared a thought for this blasted arm, but that's all changed, of course.'

'You'll have to investigate what happened in Tvøroyri in 1975.'

'That won't be easy. Kalurin is long dead, so we'll almost have to go from door to door asking. And how we're supposed to manage that, I have no idea. We can't just show up on doorsteps with a, "D'you know anything about a shackled arm?" They'll think we've lost the plot.'

'You're probably right,' I said pensively, and then it occurred to me that Edmund was supposed to look into this thing with the arm for me. Still, I didn't mention Edmund to Karl. Never hurts to have a trump card up your sleeve. If this even was a trump card. It was past eight, and I wouldn't have time to talk to Edmund tonight.

'If only that were all,' Karl sighed.

'What do you mean?'

'We're up to our eyeballs with the victim in Fagralíð, and then this arm from Beinisvørð is also haunting us. Well, probably just you and me, because no-one else has heard about it. It would be ok if that were all.'

'Spit it out. What else is there?'

Karl sort of squirmed in his plush hotel chair, there was very obviously something he wasn't happy about saying.

I scanned the restaurant, hardly an empty table, but they were all chattering away and nobody was paying the slightest attention to our conversation.

'About ten years ago a young man from Kunoy came to the station and told me that he'd seen a skeleton on the beach in a seal cave on the island. Kunoy that is. The skeleton was chained to a stone.'

9

I was dumbstruck by the revelation. We were seated at a table in the middle of the restaurant, and I looked over at the windows and out across the street to the Danish High Commissioner's mansion gleaming in the evening sun. The gulf between the hotel and the mansion's towering stone wall was deep and dark enough for the large panes to reflect the candles and diners at the window tables. Quite the cosy picture really, scuppered by the feelings that welled up inside.

I turned back to face Karl, who said: 'I think I know what's running through your head. I've barely thought of anything else since this morning, when I suddenly found myself with not just one body, but also the knowledge of potentially another two.'

I made to say something, but Karl raised his hand and stopped me.

'Let me finish, then you'll have your turn, promise.' He waved over the waiter, and when he approached ordered two cognacs and more coffee.

'I think we need it,' he said with a dark grin. 'I went straight north to Klaksvík when I heard about the body found by the folk high school students. All the way in the car my thoughts were turning over what the officer who called from the Klaksvík station had mentioned, that the man was chained to the foreshore. It brought to mind that arm in Sumba, and especially that lad from Kunoy, who claimed to have seen a chained skeleton. I just didn't know how to…'

The waiter approached with coffee and cognac, and Karl waited while he poured.

'The body on the beach was manageable. Now, don't get me wrong.' Karl held my gaze. 'It looked absolutely horrific. The eyes were pecked out, part of the nose was gone, and there was a hole in one cheek. But this was a killing that was clear-cut murder, no doubt about it. As for the arm down south, apart from the fact that it was gone, we'd sort of made our peace with it probably belonging to one of the *Westerbeek* crew.'

Karl took a swig of cognac and I did the same. He carried on: 'It was during the Ólavsøka celebrations, towards evening, that a fair-haired lad came knocking at the station. I was on duty on both days of the festival, but it had been very quiet, and the cells only held passed-out revellers we'd picked up about town. In return for working when everyone else was celebrating the national holiday, I'd be getting a whole week off, and I was sat there pondering where Katrin and I and the girls would spend it. If we should go abroad maybe, but that was ruddy expensive, and I'd be just as happy renting a house out in a village for a couple of days. Also for the girls to see another side of the Faroes than Tórshavn. The question was just which village to pick.'

Karl had some coffee and said, as he set down the cup: 'You should never rush with the coffee after cognac. Coffee and cognac straight after each other just ruins good cognac.'

I waited impatiently for him to get back on track, but held my tongue. Shortly after he continued: 'I could hear there were a few of them out in the hall, but only the blond one came inside. He was definitely not sober, and as soon as he got to the desk he blurted out that he'd seen a skeleton on the beach inside a seal cave north on Kunoy Island. And that it was God's honest truth! Then he burst out laughing, and his two or three mates in the corridor roared with laughter.

'I was in a festive mood and took it as some village boys trying to play a prank on the police. So I asked him to come back when he was sober, so we could have a chat about it. But that seemed to make him dig his heels in and he insisted that he'd told me the unvarnished truth. In early June he and a couple of mates had been north Á Gjáum, and he'd been the only one who dared venture all the way into the cave. I told him that I believed every word, but that he'd have to come back another day. Today was Ólavsøka, and we didn't care about dead men today, we were celebrating instead. This got through to him, and he told me to come shake his hand, so that we could part as true friends. Once that was done, he left and the rascals in the corridor left with him.

'I remember that after he left, I spent a moment considering whether the family should head north to Kunoy for a few days, and that's why I recall him mentioning the place name Á Gjáum. Because I looked it up on a map. In the end we didn't choose Kunoy, though, we went to Saksun instead.'

I broke my silence now: 'I get why you didn't take much note of the ramblings of a drunk youth at Ólavsøka, but it must have stung today.'

'Oh, it did, but I'm still not sure quite what to do. If there's any substance to my growing suspicion, which you've also brought up, then there's a serial killer on the loose. On the other hand, both the Sumba and Kunoy threads are gossamer-thin and it won't take much of anything to snap them. That's why I haven't mentioned this to anyone. Not until this moment.'

'Now what?' I asked.

'Well, that's precisely it. The force has its hands full with the Faroese Icelander, Ísak Joensen, and we just don't have the crew to be fumbling about in all directions. Still, we can hardly just let go of this thread. Or threads, there's more than one after all. So that got me thinking just before, if you could maybe have a look into this. You're free from most constraints and can go wherever you like. What if you tried to figure out what happened to that arm down south and maybe you could try to get a hold of that Kunoy boy.'

'Have you got his name?'

'No, unfortunately. I didn't take him seriously enough to ask for his name. But I think I remember his mates calling him Klæmint, when he went back out to join them. Then again, I can't swear to it. It could've been the name of one of the other lads, and I may also be misremembering.'

We drained our cognac glasses and left the table. When we got outside, Karl asked me, 'So, what say you, Hannis?'

'Need you really ask?' I replied.

10

Down at *Blaðið* most of the staff were at work. The body in Fa-gralíð had given them plenty to do and the atmosphere was ebullient. In the editorial room empty beer bottles crowded the tables, and that further bolstered the mood. No-one had broken into song yet, but it would hardly be long before they did.

There was no light in the managing director's office, and I stuck my head in to the editor and asked if he hadn't brought Kim Hentze in to work.

'Well, it was no walk in the park,' he laughed. 'You should've heard all the excuses. He was just about to finish the book about the airport, there were certainly no more than two hundred odd pages left, so he couldn't possibly step away from it. I asked him if he was planning to write about aviation world-wide, seeing as he needed that many pages. I also told him that it'd be good for him to come back to work for a few days, so he wouldn't completely forget what it meant to be a journalist. Then it was his car, which he'd lent his daughter, so she could drive to school up in Hoydalar. It's quite a way from Norðasta Horn where they live, you see, and it'd be difficult for him to come in on the bus. Would take much too long. I told him that his daughter could drop him off on her way to school, but he'd have none of that, I mean, then he'd have to get up before seven, and he was used to burning the midnight oil. In the end, I told him that I'd come pick and him up every morning next week, and that'll be that.'

'Impossible to get people to do a day's work nowadays,' I commented and smirked at the managing director's excuses.

'You don't know the half of it,' the editor said and got up from his chair. 'If I could only threaten to sack him, but the bastard owns plenty of shares in the paper, so that's hardly an option.'

'Hang on a minute, will you? I need a word with you.' He left for the editorial room, and I could see him standing next to a woman examining a layout on a big computer screen. They kept pointing around the screen for a while, discussing something, and then appeared to come to an agreement. With that he headed over to a young man who was typing on a computer, and spoke a few words to him. The young colleague nodded and resumed writing.

I thought to myself that most journalism was like this nowadays. You sat at a desk with a computer and a phone and barely ever left the building. Everything was done via these media. I'd never been able to work like this, and while I was free-lance, I did almost as I pleased. When I got a full-time position, I tried to take on as many municipal and parliamentary hearings, receptions for new ships and building inaugurations as possible. That way I could get out and about and partly decide myself where I spent my time. Whether I was writing about a meeting in Tórshavn or the airport west in Vágar, whether I was talking to Sandoy Island locals about the coming tunnel or the leader of a fish-filleting company in Klaksvík. I'd also taught myself to use a DSLR camera and snapped my own photos for my articles. The editor seemed reasonably happy with my work and I got by. It wasn't revolutionary reportage, but it paid my oil and electricity bills, and I had a few kroner spare to spend as I pleased.

The editor returned to the office and closed the door behind him, leaned back against it and then half-whispered to me: 'Have you found anything out about that arm with the chain?'

'I know who told me the story,' I whispered back.

'Who?'

'I won't say until I know more.'

'Bloody hell, Hannis!' he practically yelled, startling himself; he swiftly glanced over his shoulder to check if anyone next door had heard, but nobody was paying any attention. 'You work in this house, and you have to tell us what you're sodding working on.'

'I know, but I don't want what I'm starting to glimpse the outline of to be shouted on every street corner.'

'Who says it'll be shouted on every corner. I haven't told a soul about that thing you said to me. I'm no blabbermouth, no, I take pride in keeping mum,' he said quite offended.

'Come now. I wasn't trying to insult you, just to keep control of a story which could become the biggest in this paper's history.'

'Seriously?' The editor's face beamed with curiosity. ' What did you find out?'

'Best if I say no more until I know more. And I also think you shouldn't tell anyone what I said about that arm found below Beinisvørð. Not even the police know about it.' The latter was a white lie, but I knew the editor loved to have a leg up on the police. Probably because his older brother was in the force.

'I see, I see,' he rubbed his hands with glee. 'Right, we'll leave it like that then. But be quick about it for once, so we can get the whole story in the paper next weekend.'

He sat back down by his computer and, as per usual, forgot that I was there. I slipped out and went downstairs for a cup of coffee from the machine on the lower floor. A journalist from Viðareiði village passed by, and I shouted after him: 'D'you know anything about sea caves north in Kunoy?'

He looked at me as if I'd lost my marbles. 'Sea caves in Kunoy, nah, no clue about that. But there are bound to be some, the Faroes are like a Swiss cheese, pocked with caves, so why wouldn't there be any in northern Kunoy?' He headed up the staircase.

No, it was probably no use to go talking to people about geological features on a day like today. A chained corpse was all they had on their minds. I drained the plastic cup and tossed it in a bin bag propped up next to the coffee machine.

Back outside, I remembered that my car was still over by the station, because Karl and I had walked down to Hotel Hafnia. I headed up Bryggjubakki and then along Bringsnagøta crossing the oldest part of town, Reynið, with its tiny grass-thatched houses. In passing Haraldur's old house I felt a pang of longing. My plan was to head to Norðoyggjar, the cluster of islands in the north eastern corner of country, early the next day, but I was loth to go alone. I just didn't know who to ask, now that Haraldur was lounging with his wife on some island in the Mediterranean. Edmund was in hospital and, even if he were well, he would hardly be the right person to drag out to sea or into the mountains. Karl would, of course, have been an option, but though we were friends we worked in different ways. He for the police and I for the press, and they were worlds apart. On this occasion it was, in a sense, him who was sending me on an errand, but that didn't mean that I was suddenly working in law enforcement.

Then I knew a handful of the type ordinary folk would call drifters, but I couldn't quite see how they were going to give me a hand here. On the contrary. With gritted teeth I had to admit that I would have to head north on my own. Not out of choice, but because I simply couldn't think of anyone I could ask to come with me.

PEOPLE AS SHADOWS ALIGHT

Purling at the stroke of midnight
the stream softly lulls drowsing plains.
And people as shadows alight
by yards and by dew-jewelled lanes.

11

The boat sped north through Kalsoy Fjord under a blazing late afternoon sun. But there was little heat in the air, so I kept inside the wheelhouse. From the stern a small rowing boat with three thwarts, a *tristur*, was bobbing from side to side, fitted with an outboard motor.

This morning I'd driven north to Klaksvík and left the car in Biskupsstøð, the centre of town. Then I strolled along the harbour asking every person I met if they knew of anyone who could sail me to northern Kunoy. Most just replied *noy* and went on their way, but one man suggested that I try the port office, which was by Faktorsvegur. Since he could tell that I didn't know where that road was, he pointed out along the western arm of the bay. At the port office they really couldn't quite think of anyone who might take on board a *Tórshavn man*, but told me to try at the quayside at Á Stongunum, because there might be someone over there who wasn't as *local* as they were. And then they guffawed.

Over at Á Stongunum I also went around asking, but to no avail. I was beginning to think that I might have to drive to Kunoy village and ask there. It hadn't been my first instinct, because the population of Kunoy was quite small, and I wanted to draw as little attention to myself as possible. For now at least.

I was about to throw in the towel when a squat scrawny bloke in a beret approached me. He was wearing a patterned woolly jumper, blue workman's trousers and wellies. A roll-up dangled from the corner of his mouth. His face was freckled with pale eyebrows, and he must have been in his fifties. He fixed his light-blue eyes on me and said: 'Hear you're looking for a boat to take you north to Kunoy.'

'I am, yes.'

'Where in Kunoy are you looking to go? If one may ask,' he added.

'About two nautical miles north of the village. Where they say there's a gorge with a seal cave at the bottom.'

'Á Gjáum you mean?'

'Yes, that's it, Á Gjáum.'

'Know it well. Was there a lot as a lad. Grew up there, you see, in Kunoy.'

'Splendid,' I said, feeling as if fortune might finally be favouring me. 'And could you maybe sail me out to the gorge?'

The ruddy little man looked sceptical.

'I'll pay you,' I hastened to add, while frantically trying to work out in my head how much to offer.

'How about two thousand kroner?'

His expression didn't change, but he replied that it would do for the oil at least, and he didn't have anything better to do today. He told me to meet him here at the Stangabrúgv landing in an hour, he would be back with the boats.

'Boats?' I asked. 'Why would we need more than one?'

'If you're planning on looking about the cave inside the gorge, it'll have to be in a small boat, but if you're going to sail north in one of those we won't be there 'til nightfall.'

I headed to a café and got myself a sandwich while I waited. I considered bringing food along for later, but didn't think the excursion would take that long, so I dropped that idea.

One hour later I boarded a quite sizeable fibreglass boat named *Norðstjørnan*, and to its stern was tied a white rowing boat with green gunwales. The man under the beret said his name was Heini, and told me that *Norðstjørnan* could sail a good thirty miles like a breeze, but with that little one in tow, we wouldn't be clocking more than fifteen or sixteen.

I still thought it went pretty fast, because only forty-five minutes later the man who called himself Heini pointed towards land and said that there were the two gorges. He would sail up close now, so that I could jump in the rowing boat.

I could see that we weren't far south of the valley Mikladalur on the Kalsoy side, and in the fjord the sea was smooth as a ballroom floor. The little man said that we'd arrived in the calm at the turn of the tide, and to me the whole surroundings exuded utter tranquillity.

About twenty metres from shore the freckled bloke killed the engine, so I jumped in the boat and started up the motor. The bloke on board the bigger boat untied me and tossed the rope end at me with a grin.

I sailed calmly towards the gorges and entered the smaller one first, but the man had said that the seal cave was in the bigger one, so I reversed slowly out again.

Norðstjørnan had moved a little further out, and I could see that the guy on board was moving over to the side with something in his hands. That was when I was rounding the promontory separating the gorges, so I looked away and turned the boat outwards rather suddenly. In that instant something slammed into the gunwale behind me, and when I turned to look I saw white wood in the green.

I dived down in the boat, as a bullet hit the tank on the outboard motor. Luckily it didn't catch fire, but fuel was pouring out.

That bloody bastard is trying to kill me. I reared my head over the gunwale and pulled it back in the same motion. A bullet crashed into one of the boards inside the boat. That scumbag Heini was shooting at me from about fifty metres out. I grabbed the tiller and managed to turn the boat and speed up, so that we grazed past the headland. Crunching and screeching the boat scraped against the fjord cliffs to starboard, but I couldn't care less as long as it got me out of range. All the while several more bullets hit the boat, but none of them me or the motor. And then they stopped.

I risked a peek over the gunwale and could see that we were hidden from *Norðstjørnan*. But that wouldn't last long, so my only option was to head into the gorge.

It was immediately clear to me that I had to sail a distance in, out here there was enough width and height for *Norðstjørnan* to sail quite a stretch into the grotto.

I didn't dare to accelerate, so I moved inwards at half speed hoping to escape the bullets that little devil was spewing. I'd made it about two hundred metres into the gorge when I spotted the big boat out by the opening, but I didn't think he could see me. Still I flung myself down in the boat and a heartbeat later more bullets whistled through the air above me. It was clear, though, that he was firing at random.

The shots tapered off as the lit cave mouth shrank while the little boat and I sailed into the darkness.

That was when the motor died.

12

A hush descended, broken only by the murmuring of the sea and droplets bursting on its salty surface. That was all. The boat continued inwards, but ever slower, and after a while we lay still, the *tristur* and I.

The motor tank only took a few litres of petrol, and when it was perforated it had all leaked out. Luckily for me, we'd managed to get far enough into the cave that the jerk outside couldn't see us.

While the boat lay almost still, I tried to take stock of the situation. As things stood I couldn't get back out of the gorge, and unless I planned to stay right where I was, there was only one way to go, and that was further in. At the same time, I couldn't see how that would solve anything. The cave could be kilometres deep, and I would hardly find any help in there.

I could, of course, stay right here and wait. But wait for what? I had no clue. That sodding bastard, who said his name was Heini, had tried to kill me, and I didn't know why. It had to have something to do with the skeleton that the boy from Kunoy had told Karl about at Ólavsøka a decade ago. But why would that be so explosive? I had no answer.

The cave was high here and about ten metres wide, a grotto, so if I had oars I could row. There were no oars in the boat, but I thought I glimpsed a short boat-hook at the front. When I got a hold of it I could see that it was a long fishhook for hauling in catch. Well, I couldn't row with that.

How long that bloke out there would lie in wait for me was hard to say, and for all I knew he might decide to sail further in.

It was probably best to move a little further inwards, so that I wouldn't find myself staring down a muzzle before I knew it.

When the boat approached one side of the cave, I used the hook to push us further along. Progress wasn't swift, it was clumsy, but it worked. After quite a while I could no longer glimpse any daylight through the mouth of the cave and was sitting in near pitch-black dark.

Apart from plopping droplets there were no sounds. Not the engine of *Norðstjørnan* on its way in to end me either. The bloke had said that he knew the gorge well, so why wasn't he trying to sail further in?

I couldn't quite understand it, unless he knew the gorge well enough to know that he shouldn't be sailing in.

I pulled the mobile from my pocket, though I was under no illusion there would be a signal in here. Of course there wouldn't be. But I could use it as a torch, and I could see that it had a good charge. I lit a cigarette and checked my calls. A Danish number, which I recognised as Duruta's, had phoned yesterday afternoon. It was probably Turið trying to say hello to her old man. I made a mental note that I had to get used to having the sound on, not switching the phone to silent mode all the time. Sure it would vibrate when someone called while it was on silent, but given that it mostly stayed in my jacket pocket, I rarely felt that.

A Faroese mobile number had called at noon today, but that one I didn't recognise. As far as I was aware it wasn't anyone from *Blaðið* or Karl. Never mind. I also saw that I'd received a text message, and when I checked it was from Haraldur, *Hello Hannis we're in Rhodes. It's over 40 here every single day. Gasp! Beer's cold though. Greetings Sanna and Haraldur.* I could see this had arrived sometime last night, but had been sent days ago.

Different fates, eh. I was lying on board a *tristur* in a gorge in Kunoy waiting for some lowlife to shoot me, while Haraldur and Sanna were lounging on a Greek beach drinking beer. I experienced an intense urge to switch places with Haraldur.

I set the phone to battery-saving mode. Might well need it later. And then I was plunged back into darkness, which felt even blacker because of the fleeting light I'd had.

I was totally blindsided by that beret-wearing shithead, had absolutely no inkling that he might do what he did. If I made it out alive, I'd wring his neck, or worse. The question was also whether he was acting alone, and that I doubted.

For a moment I sat pondering how it all slotted together, but I was aware that I knew too little to make head or tail of anything. In this moment I had nothing better to do than to sit and think. I didn't dare to head out of the grotto. It wasn't an option for now, no matter what. And venturing deeper inside was no solution either. I did want to find out if a skeleton was lying somewhere at the end, but under the present circumstances, that had to wait. Everything had to wait. I waited.

At some point then I got the sensation that the boat was moving deeper into the cave. I pulled out the phone, switched on the torch and realised that the cave wall was moving past, at quite some speed. I pointed the shaft of light at the sea and noticed frothy wisps where the sea met the cliff.

There was a current in the gorge now the tide had turned and the lull was over. That's why the fibreglass boat hadn't sailed in, the bloke on board knew this. But how was it possible? How could there be a current inside a cave? The only answer I could think of was that there must be a hole right through the island. That the difference between high tide and low or between ocean currents on either side of the island made a river run through the gorge.

I stuffed my phone in my pocket and tried to use the hook to keep the boat away from the rockfaces. We picked up more and more speed, and I gave up on attempting to keep us off the cliffs. Instead I sat down in the middle of the boat with my mobile in one hand, ready to light up if needed.

The boat kept hitting one wall just to then lurch away and catch the other, that story repeated over and over. The cave grew ever narrower, but it was still about five metres wide. As the boat ploughed ahead, I had to sit holding onto a thwart while the sides crashed from one cliff to the next.

It was hard to assess how long this lasted, but I had no doubt that I was at least two kilometres inside the mountain by the time I felt us slowing down. I switched on the phone and lit up ahead of the bow. The grotto had widened into a proper hall, and the torch beam was far too narrow to illuminate it all. The pool in here was big, so the current was slacker, and I could see sand to port while the sea predominantly ran towards starboard. The next time the boat caught on the right side, I pushed against the wall with all my force, sending us over towards the sand. Shortly after there was no current, and when the boat came close to dry land, I leapt overboard. The sea was only up to my knees, and I pulled the bow of the *tristur* onto dry land.

I swept the sandy strip with my torch and spotted a looming boulder in the middle of it. Something pale was strewn below the rock.

I approached and found it was a skeleton with the tattered strips of some garment still clinging to it. The skull was lying at a little distance, laughing at me. Down the side of the boulder a few little bones were dangling from an iron shackle, chained to the rock.

13

As my makeshift torch lit up the bones, I considered how the young man from Kunoy never had any intention of pulling a fast one on the police, although that was what it had looked like in the end. Half-drunk and with chuckling friends in tow at Ólavsøka; you couldn't fault Karl for not believing the fair-haired youth. But why hadn't he returned once he sobered up? The only thing I could imagine was that the festive buzz had given him the Dutch courage he needed to dare pay the police a visit. Ironically, these were the precise circumstances that meant he wasn't taken seriously. Something had to explain the fact that nothing more ever came of it.

The skeleton was so far up the strip of sand that it seemed out of reach of high tides and storm breakers, so it must have been living creatures rather than the forces of nature that had been playing with the wretch. Most of the bones were strewn around the boulder, but both a thighbone and something I thought might be a shinbone were scattered a little to one side. Some animal must have sunk its teeth into the remains, but I couldn't see any seals, and birds would be unlikely to venture in here.

I walked up to the skull, and as I picked it up the jaw dropped off. It gave me a jolt, sending my heart rate up a notch. I took a few deep breaths before I examined the cranium more closely; it was completely bare. Not a trace of flesh or ligaments or skin anywhere, so it must have been lying here for years. I set it gently back down again next to the jaw.

What was left of the clothes was badly deteriorated, and I couldn't tell what material they'd been made from. Right by

71

the boulder there was something that might be reminiscent of a cap. I didn't touch anything, but I looked at the shackle where a few hand bones remained.

He who lay here was unlikely to have drowned, starvation was the most probable cause of death. Whoever had chained him to the boulder had left him sitting here alone in the pitch-dark knowing that he would succumb to starvation. His only hope would have been for a swift death. If this was a seal cave, then maybe a lone cow came to visit him many moons ago. Less comforting was the image of a bull thinking he might have encountered a rival.

I took a few steps back, thinking that the police would have to deal with this, if I ever made it out again and got hold of them. There was little doubt Karl would, sooner or later, wonder where I had disappeared to, but it could be days or maybe a week or even two, before he would send a search party this way. By then I would most likely have met my maker.

I pointed my beam of light up ahead and noticed that a little further in, to the right of the boulder, there was a stretch of pebbles. I walked towards it, and as I approached the water, I could see how the grotto on this side, much narrower than before, continued into the darkness. And it was in that direction the sea was flowing.

I switched the phone torch off and sat myself down on the sand to think in the dark. I lit a cigarette; it was the last in the pack, and it felt oddly comforting to be sitting here smoking now so much was at stake. I quit a year ago, but when Duruta and I first hit this rough patch I took up smoking again. Not a whole lot, but just as it were to have something to warm myself with.

If it had been quiet while I was lying in the boat not far from the cave's mouth, it wasn't any longer. The sea frothed through the mountain, and a distant boom resonated at intervals. Probably air being compressed and popping. The cavernous space echoed and amplified every sound, it was like being in a hall filled with maddening noise.

My attempt to gain clarity about what I should do, could do, brought me little comfort. As it was, I couldn't get out of the cave the same way I came in. The surging currents prevented that. Staying here was no solution either, I already felt pangs of hunger and though I could probably find fresh water somewhere so I wouldn't die of thirst, that was no workable future prospect either. The tidal stream wouldn't last forever, of course, but I surmised that it would be at least another four hours or so before the next lull at the turn of the tide. And there was no guarantee that would last very long. So if it was conceivable that at some point late in the evening I managed to drag myself and the boat those kilometres out of the cave, then what? I really doubted that shithead Heini would have gone home, and if he had, there would probably be someone else keeping an eye on the gorge for a few days. And this other could just as easily be waiting on land as on sea.

It occurred to me how easy it would be to pitch a tent on some tolerably flat spot near the gorge, and then two men or so could take turns for a few days checking for signs of anyone emerging from the cave. The weather was fair, and there was daylight at practically all hours, so all the odds were in their favour.

Should they feel like it, they could also at some point when the sea was calm, come in after me. It would be child's play to gun me down. Or, and this was worse, chain me to the boulder, so I suffered the same fate as my predecessor.

These thoughts did nothing to lighten my mood, but I could hardly see any other way out, unless…

I stood up again, switched on my phone light. After sitting in pitch black darkness it blinded me at first, but then I approached the cave opening that disappeared inside the mountain. Would it maybe be a possibility to be carried by the current right through the island? It was definitely risky, I hadn't a clue where exactly the rushing waters were heading. What little I saw didn't look terribly dangerous, and the stretch had to be shorter than the one I'd already travelled into the island. Kunoy is long and slender, and I seriously doubted that it was more than four kilometres across in these parts. Perhaps even just three. I estimated that the boat and I had sailed at least two kilometres in, and that meant there were no more than two left. Maybe even just one.

I left the light on and paced a few steps in each direction on the strip of sand, and every time my eyes took in the wraith by the big rock, my resolve hardened. If I wanted to avoid ending up like that poor sod, I had to get out of here as fast as possible, and there was only one way. I didn't know what lay ahead if I chose it. On the other hand, I did have an inkling what was waiting for me if I tried to exit through the gorge on the island's western flank.

Spending one to two kilometres submerged in rushing sea currents is no walk in the park. It's cold too, but there was nothing I could do about that. Instead I went over to the *tristur* and searched for something that might be of use to keep me afloat. Apart from the hook and the motor there was nothing loose in the boat, but it did have three crosspieces I could re-purpose.

Moments later I had stomped the thwarts free, and now I just had to find something to hold them together. The remnants of clothes on the skeleton were of no use, but I wouldn't be taking my jacket with me on this cruise anyway, so I tore it into strips. I was carrying a penknife, and with it I was able to fashion some usable ties, with which I then lashed the thwarts together. This wasn't exactly a lifeboat, but would hopefully serve me on the coming journey out. Finally, I took off my sneakers, which I didn't want to lose. If I got out of here alive, I had no intention of hiking across Kunoy barefoot. After tying the laces together, I hung the shoes around my neck.

Standing on the beach in my shirtsleeves and barefoot I remembered my mobile, which had been so handy as a torch up until now. I doubted that it was waterproof, but, along with my wallet and keys, I stuck it in one of my shoes and pushed everything into the toe with my balled-up socks.

For a breath I dithered; maybe I should wait until the current relented a little. But then I risked stopping in the heart of the island. That made this whitewater the better option.

I jumped in.

14

The thwarts and I were propelled into the grotto. The ride was relatively smooth at first, though I couldn't see a thing in the midnight black. Mid-stream there was a cacophony of cascading seas accompanied by a hollow rumbling. I could sense the breakneck speed and from time to time the edges of the thwarts crashed into a cliff side, sending me spinning around. It made no difference which direction I faced, there wasn't the faintest speck of light, but after what I figured were probably a couple of hundred metres, I felt the cave narrow and the currents gain force. Now I was scared that my head might hit the ceiling and I would be knocked unconscious. That would spell certain death.

In the distance I thought I could hear a gulping sound, and it was steadily growing stronger. That did nothing to allay my fear. Again and again I tried to catch hold of something on the rock face, but it was futile; there wasn't anything there to grip and the tidal stream was too strong. I managed to manoeuvre the thwarts so that we drifted sideways, and when I eventually felt a wall close in, I steered the planks diagonally towards it. This broke our speed enough for my hand to clasp a little outcrop and hold on. I pressed myself against the cliff and found a small inlet we could rest against. The slurping had become ear-splitting.

I managed to stick one hand into my sneaker with the phone and pulled it out. As I did so, both my wallet and keys fell out of the shoe. I swore, but there was little I could do. So I switched on the phone torch. Only a few metres ahead the rocky ceiling closed in completely like a lid on the water, and that was the source of the gurgling rumble.

It wasn't precisely a promising sight for me, for how long would the water run under the rock? It could be hundreds of metres and I wouldn't make it that far. I remembered from my youth how tough it was to swim just fifty metres under water. How your lungs burned in the end.

Still, it wasn't as if I had any choices to agonise over. There was only one option. I switched off and shoved the phone back into the shoe followed by the sock.

I let go of the thwarts and dived down, so I wouldn't hit the rock ceiling. I hurtled ahead at full speed, and I tried to do my bit by swimming. One minute passed, two; I knew that I could manage a little over three minutes, but then what?

It was still jet-black when my lungs started aching. Briefly I carried on, but the urge to breathe was overpowering. I began to swim upwards with one arm, while keeping the other stretched out in front to break the collision. It wasn't necessary, I half emerged from the rippling sea without feeling any ceiling.

I gasped for air like a madman, so wildly that I got brine in my mouth and into my lungs and started coughing. For a moment I drifted on the stream, hacking and spluttering, but eventually the spasms subsided. The stream also appeared to quieten, and I had the impression that the darkness wasn't quite as black as it had been. Thought I could make out contours ahead. I flipped on my back and let the current carry me out as the dark faded and the tidal stream practically disappeared.

Shortly after I glimpsed light as the mouth of the cave widened. I could also see that I was inside a gorge, which was much smaller than the one I came in through. I'd crossed through the island of Kunoy, and the stretch I'd been forced to swim under water had perhaps been quite short really. How short I would probably never know.

Out by the mouth of the gorge the shoreline began, and I hauled myself onto dry land. It wasn't until now that I wondered what time it might be. I'd pulled out my phone to use as a torch several times, but at no point had I registered what the clock said. The watch on my wrist showed that it was nearing half five. I'd spent more than three hours inside the gorge. It didn't feel like it, but I wasn't sure how long I felt I had spent in there either. In complete darkness you lose track of time and only a few hours, as in my case, seem without beginning or end. Time doesn't go by. It just *is*.

The phone was still in my shoe, but when I pulled it out it was stone dead. It wasn't made for aquatic use, but maybe it would start up again when it dried out. I shoved it in my pocket.

Now the cold hit me. I was, after all, drenched and knew that I had to move my limbs to get some warmth in my body. The sun was shining. Borðoy was shimmering gold, but not this side of Kunoy where everything was plunged in shade. Luckily I had my shoes, and when I'd pulled them on, I climbed up the hill. Not far from where I came up, there was a little stream and I quenched my thirst. Then I started to trek due south.

Though Kunoy on average has the highest summits in the Faroes, the grassy slope here just above the shore wasn't steep and so was an easy walk. And boy did I walk, so I quickly recovered my body heat.

The pressure I'd been under inside the grotto had dissipated, and I felt like singing as I half trotted south. I'd saved my own life, and to me that was worth something, though others might think it inconsequential. Maybe even that the world would be a better place without me in it making trouble. And then there were, of course, the blokes who wanted me dead. I hadn't forgotten about them, and I had to try to figure out how I would go about getting my hands on that freckled arsehole in the beret who called himself Heini.

Shortly after I reached a cluster of tumbledown houses, and when I looked up at the crags above, I could see a colossal mountain pass. I was in the abandoned village of Skarð, which I'd so often heard about at school, and about the day before Christmas Eve in 1913 when all its men of working age perished at sea, which eventually led those left behind to move away. The village had died.

Not that I stopped, I kept up my trot while thinking that Skarð was set in a stunning yet sun-starved spot. South of the derelict hamlet the terrain grew steeper and it became tougher to walk. It did occur to me, though, that there had to be a path somewhere, and when I climbed higher I found it.

Nearly two hours after I exited the cave on this side of Kunoy, I reached Haraldssund and the causeway across to Borðoy.

15

Down on the little quay in Kunoy there wasn't a soul in sight, but a red motorboat with a blue gunwale was moored at the landing. The elderly woman who had picked me up in Haraldssund, said she didn't know whose boat it was. And wouldn't I prefer a ride to Klaksvík with her?

As I'd reached Haraldssund I'd spotted this woman walking over to a red car. I approached her and asked if she could drive me to Kunoy. At first she gave me the once-over, unconvinced. Well, I wasn't a pretty sight. My clothes were dry by now, but it was clear that both they and I had seen better days.

'Goodness me, dearie,' she eventually said, 'did you fall in?'

'Yes,' I replied, 'north by Skarð village.'

'You poor thing. Come, get in the car, I'll drive you to Kunoy. I was on my way to visit my sister in Klaksvík, but no harm if she waits half an hour.'

Minutes later we were driving through the long, narrow Kunoy Tunnel. At first the woman wanted to know what I was doing up north, she could hear that I wasn't from around these parts. I told her that I'd gone on a hike to Skarð in the lovely weather, but slipped on the rocky beach and fell in. One of my friends was in northern Kunoy with a boat, and it was him I intended to get hold of.

The woman behind the wheel appeared to buy that explanation, and she switched to talking about her sister, who was married to one of the officers on one of those big Klaksvík trawlers. The sister was much younger than she was, and now that her husband was bringing home such good earnings, they were abroad travelling all the time. They could, of course, because he was only on board every other fishing trip. That was the sort of man one should have gone for, rather than that lazy git who's lounging at home on the divan. He started already complaining of a bad back when he was young, and so he's nary lifted a finger since. It's all fallen to me. She sounded exasperated. He's always saying that if it weren't for his back, he'd be a captain today. I tell him that the only thing he'll ever be captain of is the divan.

She chuckled, and I caught a glimpse of a young woman sparkling with mischief under the skin of the seventy-odd-year-old.

'If I were younger I'd have left him and found myself a real man, one who knew how to earn a bit of dosh and perhaps a few other tricks too.' She gave me a cheeky smile.

'Though I have to say that my sister's always been there for us. She gave me this car when it was only two years old. She got herself a Volvo instead. This is a Corolla. If it weren't for her, I don't know how we would've coped. The husband and I have two sons, and my brother-in-law took one of them on board the trawler, so now he's doing all right for himself too. The other one is in Denmark studying engineering, so some good will surely come of that. No thanks to my husband, mind, I can tell you that.'

All the way down to the shore in Kunoy, she went on about herself and the husband who was in such poor health. Personally, she was under the impression it was mostly down to idleness, but did add that she could also see how much pain the poor man was in sometimes. The chatter was quite innocuous overall and mostly just habit. This was her horizon.

When we parked down at the quay in Kunoy it was past eight, and I told the helpful woman that she should just head on to Klaksvík to visit her sister. She replied that she was in no hurry and intended to wait until I'd found someone to sail me.

I knew it would be dangerous to approach *Norðstjørnan*, but I thought I'd have a better chance if I didn't go alone.

Just then a dark-haired young man came down towards us and asked if he could help us with anything. I told him that a friend was in a boat north Á Gjáum, and that I wanted to head that way, and could he sail me out there?

The young bloke didn't answer my question; he pulled out a pack of shag and calmly replied with his own: 'Was it a big fibreglass boat, one of those leisure boats?'

'It was, yes.'

'Well then, you've missed the turn of the tide. It's been over an hour since I looked out the window and saw it cruising due south.' He made himself a slender roll-up, stuck it in his mouth and lit up with a match.

I quelled my urge to bum a roll-up from him, and instead said to the woman from Haraldssund that if she wouldn't mind, then I'd like to drive to Klaksvík with her.

When she dropped me off just above the Stangabrúgv landing, I very nearly knew more about her life than I'd ever wanted to know. But there's no such thing as a free ride, not even from from Kunoy to Klaksvík.

Down at the quay there was no *Norðstjørnan* in sight, so I walked north towards the Kósin fish-filleting plant, where people were still bustling. I could see a long-liner moored there, and when I approached I realised that *Norðstjørnan* was there too. I asked a forklift driver how come the fibreglass boat was moored here.

'Well, it often is,' he replied.

'Right, but what's it got to do with this fish factory?'

'The boss owns it. It's his little toy. Sky's the limit when you've got that kind of money,' and then the man drove on.

Something didn't add up. That squat bastard, Heini, definitely wasn't the company boss, but then why did he have the director's boat? I walked into the fish factory, where quite a few people were working at a filleting and washing line in a cavernous hall. Just inside the main door a small room was closed off, and on the door someone had painted: CHIEF. I knocked and stepped inside.

A large man in blue overalls was sitting with his back to me staring at a computer screen. He was greying and a round little moon was well on its way at the back of his head.

'The piece-rate seems to be holding up well, Jákup,' the bloke said and pointed a bulky forefinger at the screen.

'My name isn't Jákup.'

He swivelled around. 'Who are you?' I noticed him looking me up and down, but he didn't say anything else.

'My name is Hannis Martinsson and I work at *Blaðið* in Tórshavn. I just wanted to ask you who's taken *Norðstjørnan* out today?'

'No-one has. If they were planning to, the director has to give permission and he's in Spain negotiating salt fish sales. But why does a paper in Tórshavn want to know something like that?'

He fixed me with a searching stare, and I noticed that his overall was open almost all the way down, and underneath he was in nothing but a vest. In truth, it was hot in here.

'Right, but the boat wasn't moored here all day,' I pressed on, as if I hadn't heard his question.

'No, we moved it over to Stangabrúgv this morning, because several ships were coming in to land their catch, and I brought it back not long ago.'

'So, you just sailed *Norðstjørnan* from Stangabrúgv over here?'

'Correct, but I don't understand what this is all about. What on earth is your business with the director's boat?'

'Oh, nothing much, but a man sailed me north to Á Gjáum in Kunoy on board *Norðstjørnan* today.'

'On *Norðstjørnan*? Today? Are you sure about that?'

'Very.'

'Sounds ruddy strange. What did he look like, this man you say sailed you north to Kunoy?'

I described the guy in the beret, but the factory foreman – that's who he was – said he'd never laid eyes on a bloke like that.

'I've lived and worked in Klaksvík all my 55 years, apart from a couple when I went out sailing as a young man, so I think I know every living creature in this town.'

I noted his use of *town*, no one from Tórshavn would call Klaksvík that.

'So who can he be?' I asked of no-one in particular.

'I haven't the foggiest, but you look to me like someone who's not just been out to sea, but also in it.'

I didn't want to tell this man the whole story, so all I said was that I'd fallen in up north, and that this Heini had sailed away from me.

'Sounds to me like a very odd tale,' the foreman said, and his eyes searched me again. 'You're certain it was *Norðstjørnan* that sailed you north?'

'One hundred percent. There's no doubt.'

'Well, I don't know how this all came about, but when I have the time, I'll take a closer look at the boat. Perhaps you ought to contact the police.'

I agreed, thanked him for his time and left.

This was all getting more and more tangled, and as I strode along Nólsoyar-Pálsgøta I pondered how I would get into my car, given that I'd lost the keys. How I would then get it started, was another unknown. Well, the only thing for it was to tackle one challenge at a time.

I had spare keys at home, but the sheer thought of first going all the way south to Tórshavn for the key, and then all the way north again for the car exhausted me. I need not have worried, however, as this one issue turned out to solve itself, because where I'd left the car, there was no car. For a moment I wondered whether I was misremembering, but I recognised the spot. This was definitely it, and now the car was gone.

The bastard who shot at me knew which car I'd driven north, and seeing as he didn't think I'd survive the grotto, he'd taken the car. There was no reason for people to start speculating about a car from Tórshavn being parked in Biskupsstøð for ages.

How in the world could he know that I'd planned to come to Klaksvík? And where had he and the car disappeared to? I had no answer for either question, and so my thoughts turned to how I would get to Tórshavn. It was so late by now that the last bus was long gone. I had no money to rent a car, and I knew nobody in Klaksvík who I could ask for a lift. It was Friday night, so there would probably be lots of cars heading to Tórshavn to party, but standing by the roadside and waiting to flag down a car heading south really wasn't high on my wish list.

The police were an option, there were probably still several officers from Tórshavn here. Maybe one of them would be driving south. I knew that the station was nearby, so I walked over. When I got to the building with a sign announcing POLICE, the front door opened and out came detective Bergur Mjóvanes.

16

'What brings you up north?' asked the fair, broad-shouldered man.

Bergur Mjóvanes was second-in-command at the Criminal Investigation Department in Tórshavn and any time Karl was away he would step in to take charge. Bergur and I had often talked and were on reasonably good terms. Still, we weren't exactly friends.

'I came to ask if I could get a ride to Tórshavn with one of your cars.'

Bergur Mjóvanes turned around and looked at the police station: 'Does it say *Taxi* on their sign here in Klaksvík?' He didn't say anything while his eyes searched the façade. '*Noy*, just as I thought, it says *Police*.'

The detective was from Eysturoy Island, said '*noy*' for 'no' and spoke with a bit of a drawl. Especially when he was in the mood to goad.

'The last bus to Tórshavn left ages ago, and I've lost my wallet and keys.'

'Yeah, you look like it. Did you fall in?'

'I did. Took a tumble up in northern Kunoy, and that was when I lost my wallet and keys.'

The Eysturoy man smirked at me,

'I'll give you this, you're not a bore.' He walked over to a black Ford parked next to us. 'I'm on my way to Tórshavn, so you can ride with me. That is, of course, unless you'd rather try your luck with the cab company over there.' He nodded towards the station.

I ignored the barb and got in the car.

We sat in silence until we approached the opening of the Norðoy Tunnel and Bergur Mjóvanes asked if I perhaps felt like telling him what kind of trouble I'd been in today.

I didn't think Karl had told him about the skeleton in Sumba, or about the one hidden in the cave up north. So I attempted to cobble together a credible cover story.

'I was planning to take a look at Fagralíð from the sea, and perhaps make it on shore from there, but the arsehole who offered to take me sailed north to Á Gjáum on Kunoy instead and pushed me overboard.'

'Why in the world did he do that?' Bergur looked at me.

'Not a clue. Maybe he didn't want me going to Fagralíð.' I could hear the gaping holes in my story, but didn't know what else to say.

'He wasn't after my money, because I managed to lose my wallet all by myself.'

Bergur shot me a sceptical glance, but for a while he didn't say anything. When we emerged from the short Leirvík Tunnel and passed the village of Norðragøta shimmering in the evening sun, he asked: 'This man who pushed you overboard, who was he?'

'Well, that's what I don't know. He called himself Heini and offered to take me in a fibreglass boat called *Norðstjørnan*.'

'That boat belongs to the fish factory boss,' Bergur Mjóvanes said. 'I thought he was so attached to that craft that nobody was allowed near it.'

'I know that now. I went to the fish factory, and the foreman told me that they'd no idea that *Norðstjørnan* had been out cruising. In order to make room for the longliners due in to land their catch, they'd moved the fibreglass boat over to Stangabrúgv this morning and then brought it back this evening.'

'So this man steals *Norðstjørnan* and offers to sail you out to Fagralíð in it?'

'Precisely.'

'How did you get in touch with him?'

'I went asking around down at the landing if anyone would sail me over, and then this bloke came and offered his services.'

'And then you boarded *Norðstjørnan* with him?'

'Not immediately. We agreed to meet an hour later, and at that point he was moored at the landing with the boat.'

'Impressive,' laughed the detective, 'what a joker. First he steals a boat and then he pushes you overboard. But why?'

'I've no idea.'

'Right…' This one little word dripped with disbelief.

We drove another stretch in silence, but as we crossed the Gøtueiði Pass Bergur Mjóvanes asked me: 'How did you get to Klaksvík today? Did you catch the bus?'

'No, I came in my car, but it's vanished. I'd left it by the police station, but there was no car there any more.'

'I'm speechless. Grand bunch of friends you've got. First they steal a boat, then they shove you in the water, and then they make off with your car.' There was a sardonic laughter in his voice.

'That was no friend of mine. I've never seen him in my life,' I tried to protest. I was aware, however, that there were as many holes in my story as there were gorges in the Faroe Islands, and so I left it at that.

'So what did this not-friend-of-yours look like?'

I told the detective about the squat man in a beret, patterned woolly jumper and wellies. And also that he was freckled, had pale eyebrows and lashes and was in his fifties.

'That describes many a man, but I'll look into it when we get south.'

I thought we'd talked more than enough about me and my adventures, so I asked: 'What about the guy who was shackled on the foreshore, do you know anything?'

'Oh, we've figured a couple of things out, but if you're here as a journalist, I can't say much, now can I?'

'I've taken a two-week leave, so nothing you tell me here will be in the paper. At least not for the coming two weeks.'

'That should do. Hopefully we'll have caught the perpetrator by then.' The car drove into the Eysturoy Tunnel as Bergur

Mjóvanes told the story: 'The victim's name was Ísak Joensen, we finally found out, and he was from Klaksvík. He hadn't lived in the Faroes for the last half century. It wasn't until we asked at a care home that people recognised him, saying that they'd heard he lived in Iceland.'

I didn't breathe a word about the fact that Karl had already informed me the body was that of one Ísak Joensen. As far as I was concerned it was a matter of lying low and saying as little as possible.

'At first when we checked with the Icelandic authorities we were told that there was no Ísak Joensen in their registers. That was when a bright spark at the station flagged up that any-one seeking naturalisation as an Icelandic citizen is required to have an Icelandic name. And so we tried with Ísakur Jónsson, and we had better luck. It turned out that Ísakur Jónsson lived in Ytru Njarðvík near Keflavík, that he was an engine mechanic on an Icelandic longliner and had been an Icelandic citizen for almost forty years.'

'You say he was an engine mechanic when he died?'

'Correct.'

'But he was past seventy.'

'Ah, but the Icelanders don't have a fixed retirement age. Unless they're sent home, they carry on until they kick the bucket. Ísakur Jónsson was still sailing on the longliner *Hekla*.'

We stopped at the petrol station by the bridge, because Bergur needed the toilet, and I went in intending to buy myself a pack of cigarettes. That's when I remembered that I had no money on me, so I turned back to the car and got in.

A moment later we continued on our way to Tórshavn.

'It would appear that Ísak Joensen fled to Iceland, and that he more or less hid there,' Bergur Mjóvanes carried on. 'He left Klaksvík in 1955 and until now he hadn't been back to visit the Faroes. That's what the care home residents said, and just this afternoon they called from Iceland. They'd been to Ytra Njarvík to have a chat with people who knew Ísak and who said that he was friendly and quiet. Someone who's sailed with him for years told them that they docked in Faroese ports fairly regularly, but that Ísakur never wanted to go ashore. He also refused to speak of his old homeland.'

'Can't it just be a case of burnt bridges? Maybe he was in love with a girl who left him, and that sent him running to Iceland.'

'We made enquiries in that vein at the care home, but none of the people who knew him were aware of anything that might have made him run away. Suddenly one day he was gone, and no-one in Klaksvík had seen him since.'

'So why did he come now?'

'Hard to say. Maybe he was getting on and yearned to see his home village one last time. We haven't managed to suss out if he visited anyone. He'd booked a room at the sailors' lodgings, Sjómansheimi, in advance, and he also took his meals there.'

'Ísak Joensen vanished for no discernible reason in the mid-1950s, and he returned just under a week ago. Also for no discernible reason. And on the night between Sunday and Monday he was shackled on the shore in Fagralíð and drowned. There has to be something behind it.'

'Of course there is, but we have no inkling what exactly. Nobody we've spoken to has been able to give us any leads at all.'

'What about the crime scene, have you found anything there?'

'Nothing but dead ends so far, which in itself is odd. On Monday night a man was shackled to the shore and all he could do after that was sit and wait for the tide to rise. As far as I've understood, this happened early Monday morning. So until Thursday morning his body was left as an open banquet for birds and others who fancied a nibble, and he looked like it. There may not be people in Fagralíð every day, but we're nearing high summer, and the spot isn't far from built-up areas, so it seems a little bizarre that nobody had seen a thing. That it took a folk high school class from Tórshavn to find the man.'

We passed Hvítanes as the detective offered this stark conclusion, and though we shortly after could take in Tórshavn in a blazing sunset, we both sensed that something sinister was asserting its power.

17

My plan was to go home and get changed, and I was hungry too, but Bergur Mjóvanes was crafty. He insisted it would be best if I came with him to the station, where I could have a word with Karl, tell him my story. That way I could also give the traffic department my licence plate number, in case they came across my car, you see. His delivery was deadpan, but I saw the little smile playing at the corners of his mouth. I had to play along, there was nothing else for it.

Over at the station the same young woman officer was manning the reception desk, and I gave her the car's make, model and licence plate number. She promised to pass the information along.

The top corridor was crowded with people coming and going from the offices, and Karl was discussing something with a couple of men in his. Bergur Mjóvanes poked his head inside and told him that he'd brought in a man who had a story to tell. Then he left.

I waited in the corridor, and when Karl had finished with the pair, he told me to come in and shut the door behind me. I did as I was told.

Karl looked exhausted and he rubbed his eyes a moment, then scratched his cheek, before saying: 'What have you landed yourself in now, seeing as Bergur is adamant that you have a story to tell me? Does it have anything to do with the grotto Á Gjáum?'

'It does, but I wasn't sure how much I could share with Bergur Mjóvanes, so I could only paint him half a picture.'

'Don't worry about that. I'll deal with Bergur. Go on, tell me what you found up north.'

For a good half hour I was telling Karl the whole story about the man who called himself Heini, and about my odyssey in the underworld, and about the shackled skeleton on the strip of sand, and about how I made it out again on the other side of Kunoy. I concluded with a recap of how the blokes at the fish factory didn't know their boat had been taken for a joyride, and that my car was gone too.

When I finished Karl was lost in thought for a moment, while I sat there wondering where I might get a bite to eat.

'Are you hungry?' he suddenly asked.

'Could eat a horse.'

'The kitchen is open tonight. I can ask them to make you a couple of open sandwiches and bring them up here.'

I told him how bloody marvellous that would be, and Karl took the phone and ordered three sandwiches and two cups of coffee. Then he gave me an inquisitive look.

'So, if I've got this right, you reckon that the squat freckled bugger has been on your heels all the way from Tórshavn.'

'Right, otherwise how would he know what car I drive?'

'Could it not be by chance? He happened to be in Biskupsstøð and saw you arrive?'

'You don't believe that yourself, Karl. Of course chance might play a role, it often does, but not in that way. It's been the plan from the beginning that I have to be stopped, but I just don't get why. No attempt was made to conceal the body on the beach in Fagralíð. So why would they want to prevent me from entering the gorge in Kunoy and finding the skeleton there? It makes no sense. How things stand with the bones from down south, we obviously don't know, but I'd be really surprised if they weren't part of these machinations.'

We looked at each other, and Karl said: 'Nobody but us knew that there was supposed to be a skeleton in a cave at Á Gjáum in Kunoy. Well, apart from that young bloke from Kunoy who came to me a decade ago. But he's hardly involved in this game,' he said pensively. 'Or?' Karl paused for a moment and then continued: 'I didn't know you were planning to head up north today either. You could just as well have gone to Suðuroy. It's all very odd. Are you sure that man was trying to kill you?'

'Of course I'm bloody sure. He fired several shots at me.'

I'd raised my voice, and Karl said: 'All right, Hannis, calm down! I believe you, but I just can't make head or tail of all this.'

As he said it the door opened and the receptionist came in, carrying a tray with a plate and two mugs.

'All we had left was cheese,' she said with a smile. 'Everything else has been gobbled up, now there are so many people here. Hope that's ok?' She looked at me and set the tray down on Karl's desk.

'That's great. I love cheese,' I said and reached for the first slice of rye bread.

The young woman left the office and the pair of us sat in silence while I devoured the sandwiches. Karl was drinking his coffee and I was doing the same, when something sprang to mind.

'Edmund West!' I said so suddenly that it startled Karl.

'What about him? Isn't he in hospital with some kidney trouble?'

'Yes, but I visited him yesterday and asked him about the arm that was found down south. This was before I came to see you. Edmund said he'd never heard of it, he was studying in Denmark when there was that rockslide on Beinisvørð, but he promised to look into it.'

I pulled my phone out of my pocket, but it was just as dead as before.

'Before this thing shut down, I noticed a missed call from an unknown number this morning. That could have been Edmund using the phone at the hospital.'

'What has Edmund West got to do with the events today?'

'Nothing and everything,' I replied to the baffled detective inspector.

18

The taxi dropped me off at the entrance to the National Hospital. Karl had lent me a few hundred kroner, and we'd agreed that it probably wasn't the worst idea for me to head out here and have a word with Edmund. Should whoever was trying to bump me off have received their information via Edmund, there was no telling as to whether they would come after him too. Karl thought it unlikely, though, and he didn't want to post a manned car at the hospital to keep guard over one of my drinking buddies, as he put it. Wouldn't surprise me if Katrin or Duruta had a role in that word choice.

There didn't seem to be anyone in the hospital foyer, and that suited me just fine, given how late it was. Visiting hours were long over, and I had little appetite for getting into an argument with some busybody trying to prevent me from getting up to the ward.

I took the lift up to the inpatient medical ward, where I briefly wondered why the nurses' office was empty. As far as I knew, there was always meant to be someone on call in this ward, but perhaps they were in one of the rooms?

Gently I opened the door to Edmund's room, and found him reading in his bed. The bedside lamp was on, and his glasses balanced on the tip of his nose. When he noticed me, he put down his book and said: 'Blimey, a midnight drop-in at the hospital, ye don't get that every day. Might ye be looking for someone to share a tipple?' He flashed a broad smile.

'No, that wasn't why I came, though I could also use someone to raise a glass with.'

Edmund looked me up and down: 'The state of ye! Have ye been swimming with yer clothes on?' His Suðuroy lilt emphasised the word *clothes*.

'Nah, I forgot to undress before getting in the shower,' I replied, but immediately added: 'It's a long story, which I'll tell you in a minute. But first I need you to answer a couple of questions.'

'Not hard to tell ye've been shacked up with someone from the station all these years. It's do as ye're told, or else…'

'Bollocks, Edmund. This is serious,' I cut him off. 'Did you find anything out about those arm bones I mentioned?'

Edmund sat up a little in the bed. 'Aye, I think I did. Tried to call ye this morning, but ye didn't pick up.'

'No, I was otherwise engaged. And?' I quizzed him.

'The old cousin down south was puzzled by ma question at first, but said he recalled the arm, though not a soul had breathed a word about it in these thirty odd years. As far as he knew, those bones were still tucked away in his basement in Trongisvágur.'

'What?' I blurted out. 'Are those bones lying in the basement of his house?'

'Aye, for now. He told me that his children had been trying to sell the house ever since he moved into a care home, but they hadn't managed yet. So he just figured that the bones were still where he put them way back when.'

'How did he get hold of the bones? I mean, they were in the boot of Kalurin's car.'

'It wasn't Kalurin's car, you see. It belonged to the squad, and when he, dad's cousin, was going on duty he set about washing that vehicle inside and out. He told me he nearly always had to after Kalurin used it, because he was such a slob. In the boot he found the canvas bag with the bones in it, and though he thought it looked like a human arm, he simply carried the bag into the basement and left it up on one of the exposed beams. His intention had been to return the bag when he passed the car over to Kalurin again the following week, but it had slipped his mind. No-one had ever asked for that bag of bones, and although over the years he'd come across it again a couple of times in the basement, he'd never done anything about it. It was already crammed with clutter, and by then he was too old to bother with clearing out. His heirs could do that, he concluded.'

'But he didn't know anything about the arm being from the Beinisvørð foreshore?'

'I enquired about that, but he'd never heard anything to that effect. He also insisted that, seeing as he knew nothing of it, it probably didn't happen,' Edmund chuckled. 'That geezer never thought too little of himself.'

'Well, it still doesn't make him right on that count,' I said, 'because I got this story from Karl Olsen. And he was with Kalurin in Sumba in person when they picked up the arm.'

'Right, I see. Interesting,' Edmund said in a pensive tone.

I thought I could hear footsteps in the corridor, but when I strained my ears there was nothing.

'What about yerself, how did ye end up in that state?'

I gave Edmund a brief summary of the whole story, right back to when Karl and Kalurin were in Sumba all those years ago and up until this point with me sitting there on a stool by his bedside.

When I'd finished, Edmund laughed. 'Well, ye've done Faroese folklore research a great service. Ye've proven a tale that tells of a milkmaid dropping a covered milk pail into the sea Á Gjáum, which was found again the next day in the gorge of Gjóðardalsgjógv, next to Skarð, where there's also meant to be a seal cave. It's an old belief up north that there's a hole right through the island, but nobody had ever found it before.'

'Well, there may never have been anyone wedged quite so tightly between a rock and a hard place up there,' I replied dryly.

After a little while Edmund said: 'So, ye figure that the bloke who was out to get ye, somehow sniffed out that ye were heading north in search of skeletons, and that he was on yer heels.'

'I don't know,' I said. 'Something along those lines I suppose. It's already hard enough to make head or tails of any of this, so if that's the case maybe it would help explain it.'

'Perhaps, but I've a hard time seeing how, on account of me talking to that pensioner at the care home down south, some-one up here is supposed to have found out and started follow-ing ye.'

'I know,' I said. 'It's all clear as mud, but I'm convinced that the bloke in the beret wasn't in Klaksvík by chance.'

'No, I can see that, but other than that there's not much rhyme or reason to everything that's going on. That Karl and ye think that my life's somehow in peril is also far-fetched. I mean, I haven't a clue about any of this.'

'You know as much as I do, and that prick tried to murder me.'

'Aye, but ye're a journalist poking yer nose in here and there, while I'm washed up in hospital letting medics run tests on me. Who could I possibly be a threat to?' Edmund looked at me with eyes full of questions.

'I don't know, and I don't know who I'm supposed to be a threat to either. But there's some piece of information that the person in question wants to keep from getting out, and the cost of that would appear to be irrelevant.'

'I can't fathom what's the secret here. Ísak Joensen was killed completely in the open. The radio broadcast his identity tonight, and that he was shackled is also public knowledge.'

Again I thought I could hear something out in the corridor.

I raised a finger to my lips, signalling to Edmund to hush, and whispered, 'There was no one at the reception when I came, and no one at the nurses' station in this corridor. Is there any way to lock the door in here?'

I scanned the door. It didn't have a lock.

'There's a wedge on the floor, right up by the wall beside the door,' Edmund whispered back. 'The porters use it when they want the door to stay open.'

I went over and spotted a grey plastic wedge, which I pushed under the door right below the door handle.

I signalled to Edmund to switch off his reading lamp and that left us waiting in semi-darkness. Beneath the door a sliver of light showed through from the corridor.

A few minutes ticked away, and I was beginning to wonder if I'd been spooked by trolls when a shadow moved across the slender beam of light. Then the door handle was pushed down, and something tried to push the door open, but the wedge held it shut. The door handle swung back up. But the shadow was still blocking the light.

It was dead still. Both in the room and in the corridor. Then the handle slowly moved down again, and there was another push at the door. The wedge was as firm as stone.

Moments later the shadow disappeared and cautious steps receded down the corridor. Then a door slammed.

'That's the door to the staircase,' Edmund whispered. 'It slams all day, because the staff prefer it to the lift. It's quicker. But in the evening and at night ye don't usually hear it.'

'Seems like someone doesn't want to be seen,' I whispered back.

We sat in silence for a couple of minutes, then I went over to remove the wedge and opened the door a crack. I poked my head out, but there wasn't a soul. I closed the door and told Edmund that he could switch on the lamp.

'I doubt that devil will return tonight, but he might try again another day.'

'I'll be damned,' Edmund said. 'That was eerie, but I find it hard to believe he was coming to murder me.'

'Believe what you will. Whoever it was his intentions were no good, if they were he would've asked us to open the door.'

'What am I supposed to do here, bedridden and tethered?' Edmund raised his left arm and showed me a needle with a tube dangling from the crook of his arm, which attached him to a bottle hanging from a steel frame. 'I have to take this with me, even to go to the loo.'

'Hopefully I or the police will figure this out soon, so that it'll be over with, but until then you'll have to watch yourself. Whoever was here will hardly come back in the daytime with so many people around, but likely at night. Before going to sleep, you'll have to shove the wedge under your door, so he can't get at you.'

'My home is my castle,' Edmund chortled, and in that instant the door swung open and the young redhead entered.

'What on God's green earth are ye doin' here?' She glared at me, making it perfectly clear that I was out of bounds. 'D'ye have any idea what time it is?'

I checked and noted that it was nearing midnight.

'Hannis just stopped by to tell me something. He couldn't come earlier and ye know I stay up late reading anyway.' He raised the book he'd been reading when I arrived. I could see that it was a tome on Faroese folklore, *Sagnir og Ævintyr* by Dr Jakobsen.

'That's fine and ruddy dandy, but we cannae have people without any business here come runnin' at all hours.' She was clearly placated, though, and gave Edmund a smile.

'You didn't meet anyone in the corridor when you came just now, did you?' I asked.

'Ye mean someone who isnae supposed to be here?'

I concluded that she had the brains to match her beauty.

'Yes,' I replied.

'No, I dinnae, but something very odd happened tonight.' She approached the bed.

'Half an hour ago both the reception staff and the two of us on shift here on the ward were notified that we were bein' called to the surgical ward immediately, because they needed help. Except when we got there, nobody was around. We found the doctor on call, but he was asleep in the on-call room, and was completely oblivious. Nothin' had happened since he signed in to his shift in the afternoon, and he insisted he hadnae called for anyone.' She looked at us both with a grave expression: 'Beggars belief that anyone would play pranks at a hospital. It could cost lives.'

'Indeed it could,' I replied with a knowing look at Edmund.

19

The next morning I was woken by the ringing of the phone on the bedside table. It was Bergur Mjóvanes.

'Morning Hannis. Sleep well?'

'Mm, I did, and still would be, if you hadn't called and woken me at this hour.'

'This hour! It's half past nine, and the sun is out. Rise and shine.' He laughed down the line.

'I'm guessing this isn't a courtesy call to give me the time and the weather report.'

'Nah, that's not why I called. It's to tell you that you won't be needing to look for your car. It's been found.'

'Well, that's great,' I said. 'Did you find it round these parts?'

'No, it was parked in a lay-bay in the Árnfjørður Tunnel. That's the first tunnel out of Klaksvík heading north.'

'Funny place to leave the car,' I mused.

'So it is, but you'll also have to consider changing the upholstery on the driver's seat.'

'How so?'

'Because it's drenched in blood.'

'Drenched in blood?' I was dumbfounded.

'Oh, did I forget to mention?' The detective feigned innocence. 'That beret bloke of yours was in the seat and someone had slit his throat. Over a litre had leaked out onto the seat. Hard to believe there could be that much blood in such a small man.'

In silence I pictured the short freckled man sitting in my car with a gaping throat. It wasn't precisely a soothing image.

'We need you to confirm if this is the same man who sailed you north to Á Gjáum instead of Fagralíð.'

I could tell from his tone that he knew what had happened. Karl must have told him.

'Look, I'm sorry I didn't tell you the whole story yesterday, but I'd agreed with Karl…'

'Never mind, never mind,' Bergur Mjóvanes cut in. 'I never trust a word journalists say or write anyway. Still, it wouldn't do any harm if you occasionally tried telling the truth.'

He paused, and I thought it best to keep my mouth shut.

'Be at the National Hospital in an hour, your driver should be here by then.' He was just about to hang up, when I interjected: 'The bloke in the beret, when did you find him in the car?'

'I don't have all the details, but the colleague from the station up north who I spoke to said that the car has been parked in the lay-by since last night. An auditor from Viðareiði was working late yesterday and saw the car standing there on his way home. On his way back to work this morning, he spotted the car in the same place, so he pulled over to check what the problem might be. And what *that* was quickly became crystal clear,' Bergur explained and hung up.

I was sitting on my bed trying to get the image of the man in the beret out of my mind, but it wasn't easy. At the same time, it was clear to me that if this man was killed last night, maybe shortly after he'd taken my car, then he hadn't been at the hospital late last night at all.

For the last couple of days I'd been suspecting that there was more than the one person involved in this affair. But who they might be, I hadn't the faintest idea.

20

At the car dealership in Hoyvík they'd been a bit reluctant to rent me a car for what I wanted to pay. They told me it was peak tourist season, and why didn't I buy a used car instead. I said that I had a car, but just couldn't drive it right now. In the end they gave me an old Ford Mondeo, which I could rent on the cheap. It had been for sale for nearly two years, but since it had been a cab, nobody wanted to buy it. As soon as I sat in the car, it felt like I'd wound up on the floor. Not a spring was left in the seat. Though the salesmen protested and grumbled that it was Saturday and impossible to find a mechanic at the workshop, I got them to swap the two front seats. And that helped.

At the hospital I'd identified the freckled little man as the person who sailed me north to Á Gjáum, and confirmed that he'd fired shots at me. His face was literally pale as a corpse, and a crimson line ran under his chin. I told the officer who took my statement that it must have been one hell of a sharp knife. He said he wasn't at liberty to disclose anything to me. Not even who he is? I tried asking, and the answer was, no.

I was on my way over to the SMS shopping centre now to get a new mobile phone and a bite to eat. As per usual on Saturdays it was heaving, and I had a hard time getting rid of the car, but in the end I found a place down in the parking basement.

In the phone shop I asked a young shop assistant for a cell phone with a torch, and it made him laugh.

'What century did you last buy a mobile phone?'

'I don't know, a few years back,' I replied, feeling a little miffed.

'It's been years since mobiles with torches were on sale.' He headed over to a wall with row after row of phones.

'Wouldn't you like a smart phone for just 5,500 kroner for the first six months?'

I declined, and asked for a plain regular phone, which you can use to make calls and send text messages. When I showed him the mobile that had been in the sea with me, he said that the last time he'd seen one of those was in year 7 at school. He was helpful, though, and in the end I bought a phone for only five hundred kroner. He said that the SIM card from the old phone was probably usable, even though the rest of the electronics were shot. And he was right.

Moments later I was sitting in a restaurant by the little shopping centre plaza, Torgið, eating a sandwich with a cup of coffee, when a shadow fell across my table. I looked up and straight into the face of Judith Christiansen, the nurse I'd been with after the Christmas party at *Blaðið*.

'How are you, Hannis?'

She fixed me with her melancholy hazel gaze. With her brown curls and symmetrical features, she was just as beautiful as I remembered her.

'Oh, I'm all right,' I replied, a little uneasy. 'Would you like to sit down?' I asked after a pause.

She looked away and I could see that she was carrying a shopping bag from the Miklagarður supermarket in each hand. Then she turned back towards me and said: 'Yeah, for a bit perhaps, if you can get your hands on a cup of coffee. I'm lugging so much stuff that I…'

'Of course,' I replied and went over to the counter. The queue was on the long side, so it took a while before I returned with her cup.

At first neither of us said a word; I ate the rest of the sand-wich and Judith sipped her coffee. After a while the quiet became almost embarrassing, but I didn't know what to say. That was when Judith broke the silence.

'There's something I've been wanting to tell you for a long time, Hannis.' She looked down at the table, as if she were ashamed. 'It's about my panties. God knows I did look for them, but I had to rush home, because I'd promised to drive one of my sons to the airport. He was going to Denmark to spend Christmas with his dad who now lives in Esbjerg. Had I known that you and Duruta…'

'So you know what happened?'

'Yeah, I know now. At first I was quite upset with you for being so awkward on the phone when I called. But later I heard that Duruta found my panties behind the toilet, and that she ended things with you.'

'So it's common knowledge?' I asked in a mordant tone.

'No, no, not at all,' Judith protested. 'You know that I work at the care home Lágargarður with Katrina and Karl's daughter, and one day she told me that a friend of her mum's had found a pair of black panties behind her boyfriend's toilet. She also told me that this friend had moved to Denmark in a fit of rage, and taken her daughter with her.'

Judith looked me in the eyes. 'The rest wasn't hard to guess.'

We said nothing until Judith carried on, 'I had no idea that you and Duruta were still together. I knew you had been, and that you had a daughter with her, but I thought it was over long ago.'

'Well, in a way it was, and yet…' I paused briefly. 'When you don't live together and one of you moves to Denmark for a year and practically only yells at you when you're on the phone with her, then I guess it doesn't take much.'

'For you to sleep around.' It was a statement from Judith, not a question.

'Yes and no.' I was squirming a little, but tried to explain, 'I really liked you. Really like you,' I added. 'But Duruta is the mother of my daughter, and we've been together for quite a few years. So when they come home to visit for Christmas and Duruta has let her house, then it's a given that they come and stay with me. The problem is just whether Duruta and I have interpreted our relationship in the same way. I'd understood that we were nearly done with each other, but she was obviously thinking that we'd carry on. That's where the misunderstanding, or whatever you might call it, stems from.'

'Are you calling my panties a misunderstanding?' Judith smiled, and I had to smile back.

'No, I don't think it was any misunderstanding that you spent that night at mine, but it caused quite the ruckus.'

Judith touched my hand and said, 'Well it's great to have a word with you at least. It's always upsetting to go around brooding on something.'

I nodded in agreement and felt a warmth seep through my body. It was as if the two of us were in our own little world in the midst of the Saturday noon SMS maelstrom.

'Well, just look who's sitting here!' A voice cut into the moment, and the din of the crowd and clinking of porcelain were suddenly audible at full volume.

It was Haraldur and by his side, Sanna. They were both tanned and looking very jolly.

We all exchanged greetings, then Judith said she had to run and took my hand. 'See you around, Hannis,' were her parting words of promise.

'She's good-looking, that one,' Haraldur remarked, following Judith with his gaze as she headed for the exit to the parking lot.

'Hey! No ogling other women,' Sanna joked. 'You've got enough with me.'

'Right you are, milady,' Haraldur said, wrapping his arm around Sanna's waist.

Standing there, they were a glowing epitome of ageless love. Haraldur was stout, his black hair and beard liberally streaked with grey, and his eyes sparkling blue, while Sanna was a little plump with brown hair and lively dark eyes. Haraldur was pushing sixty, and Sanna was only a few years younger, but they were like teenagers together.

They sat down at my table and I asked: 'What on earth are you doing here? I got the text message you sent from Rhodes only a couple of days ago. And I was under the impression that the honeymoon would last for months?'

'That was the plan,' Haraldur said, 'but when you've been away in the heat for over a month, the fun starts to wear off.'

'It also gets boring, when you've got nothing to do,' Sanna added. 'Just taking time off day after day, week after week, it's exhausting.'

I had to laugh. 'I think it was an Englishman who once said that a perpetual holiday is a good working definition of hell.'

'Very nearly,' Haraldur smiled. 'But it's not that we've given up on travel. We're just going to divvy it up into shorter stints.'

'In October we'll have a week in Mallorca,' Sanna explained, 'and after Christmas I expect we'll go to Thailand.'

'As long as it isn't as hot as it was in Rhodes, I'm up for it,' Haraldur said and kissed Sanna.

And I felt a pang of jealousy, but was also happy for them, and to have Haraldur back. He was like a rock in swirling currents, and you could always find yourself in need of a man like that.

Dusk-giddy Puffins Still Calling

The mountain slumbers in silence,
dusk-giddy puffins still calling.
Now an ocean dozes in stillness.
To rest the flocks are withdrawing.

21

It was an old red timber house with a painted white cement foundation. Built at some point in the 1920s or 30s and much like so many houses from that period. White curtains were draped in the windows upstairs, but there wasn't a flowerpot in sight, a sure sign that nobody lived there. Or that it was a bachelor's lair, come to think of it.

I'd travelled on the four o'clock afternoon ferry, and on the crossing south I asked after the house belonging to Edmund's father's cousin. The talkative lady I shared a table with on board had enquired whether I was wanting to buy the house. I told her that I didn't think so, though I'd promised a friend to find him a house in Tvøroyri. Then my tablemate wanted to know who this friend was, and what he would be doing in the village. She very nearly had me trip up in my cover story; I rescued myself by saying that I'd promised not to tell anyone who he was, but that he was planning to set up a new company in the south. This steered the lady's chatter on to the old days, when Tvøroyri was a bustling village. Her parents had told her about the years when Suðuroy was the leading light of entrepreneurship in the Faroes, and when as much as a third of the population lived here. I was well versed in the history of the island, which had ploughed ahead with the emergence of ocean fisheries, but had since become a backwater. The population was dwindling and the industry with it.

As I drove ashore at Krambatangi Ferry Port and turned right towards Trongisvágur village, I had first considered finding the care home where the retired officer now lived, and asking his permission to retrieve the bones from his basement.

But the old house was practically on the road from the ferry port, and I didn't think he would mind me taking the remains of an arm. Of course I knew you couldn't just walk into people's houses without permission, but I comforted myself with the thought that then the old man's heirs wouldn't have to dispose of these remains.

The green basement door wasn't locked, and I stepped across the high threshold. It was dark inside and the ceiling low enough that I could walk under the beams, just. I located one of those bulky brown switches and flicked on the light. A weak bulb dangled naked from the ceiling and cast an eerie light on the basement, which was the incarnation of an era. An old oil-fired boiler was right inside the door, but it was off. Everyone knew it was a bad idea to leave the heating off completely, but this contraption probably dated back to right after the Second World War. As I recalled, they had a habit of going off all the time, and if no-one was looking after the house, then it wouldn't be turned back on.

All manner of clutter crammed every corner of this basement. There were long line vats, left for so long that they'd very nearly fossilised, a washing machine with a mangle on the side for wringing the laundry, and handlines in varying sizes crowded the walls. Brooms, shovels and spades were lined up along the wall, and in the middle of the floor stood a sizeable grindstone. At the far end were the vestiges of a stall with a manure channel, so once upon a time a cow had been kept in this house. Crossbeams were nailed across the exposed beams and along these stretched bamboo fishing rods and some scythe-handles, but I couldn't see the canvas bag, which was meant to be there too.

I ran my hand along the beams, but there was no bag to be found. Then I spent a good while searching the entire basement, and though many an ancient artefact came to light, I didn't unearth the bones of the arm found by Sumba men below Beinisvørð.

I backed up against the door and scanned the basement. Had I gotten the house wrong? No, I didn't think so. The lady on board the ferry *Smyril* had been very clear, and I'd seen that both the neighbouring houses were lived in. So how was this possible?

Only late last night Edmund had told me that his father's cousin back in the day had taken the canvas bag from the car and shoved it up among the beams. He'd also said that he expected it still to be there. I didn't know how long he'd been in the care home; one of his children could, of course, have found the bones and have either thrown them away or buried them. I doubted it, though, because it didn't look as if anyone had been here to clear out since the old man moved.

Could the former policeman be misremembering? Could he have left the bones somewhere else in the house? Also unlikely, because according to Edmund he was sharp as a tack, in spite of his age. Perhaps I should check the beams one more time.

I could have used my old phone torch right now, but I went out to look for an alternative in the car. There was none in the glove compartment and nothing in the side door pockets. So I searched the boot, then lifted the rubber boot carpet and looked around the spare wheel recess, where I found the wheel-changing tools stuffed in a black bag. It had a little workshop light in there of the kind you can stand on the ground to light up the area you're working on. Just what I needed.

Back inside I found a low stepstool to stand on, while I swept the beams with the light to see if the canvas bag with the bone relics wasn't there somewhere after all. Moments later I'd searched most of the space, all that was left was the segment above the cow stall. That's when I saw them, the footprints in the dust on the cement floor.

I moved closer and pointed the light in that direction. The contour of a shoe with a patterned sole crisscrossed most of the floor inside the stall. Something else had also made a pattern in the dust. Something had been dragged along the floor, and I could see that it was a short bench. I stepped up on the bench and lit up the crossbeams where some boards had been laid.

In the middle of the boards there was nothing, not even dust.

22

Someone had come for the bag of bones, but who the hell knew it was here? In a way this pointed back to Edmund West, who appeared to be in some pivotal position in relation to the bloke who came after me north to Klaksvík, as well as the now vanished canvas bag. I just couldn't suss out the connection. Edmund certainly hadn't given up this information deliberately. I abandoned that train of thought.

A staircase, more of a ladder really, led up to a trapdoor near where I was standing. A quick glance at what the upstairs looked like couldn't hurt. I was already on such intimate terms with this property, that it would hardly make much of a difference if I went upstairs too.

First I listened for a while, but there wasn't a peep from the house. Nor from the road. So I climbed in through the trapdoor and found myself in a little entry. A steep staircase led up to the top floor and there were three white doors, in addition to the front door. The first I tried opened into a minuscule room with space for nothing but a narrow bed. Other than that it was empty.

The next door revealed a front room and I stepped cautiously inside. Here was a sofa, armchair and sofa table with a bowl on a crocheted doily. In a corner stood an old-fashioned TV set. Most of the wall was concealed by photos, and a closer look revealed wedding pictures, snaps of ship crews and police officers, scattered in a crowd of portraits featuring near and dear unknown to me. A framed diploma announced that the man of the house had received the 'Silver Medal for Merit' for forty years of service in the police force. I remembered hearing someone say that if you worked the same job for that long, you shouldn't be getting a medal, but a fine.

From the front room there was a door to what was clearly the living room. Here was a dining table with chairs around it, a sideboard with a clock on top and a short bookshelf. On the shelf there were only two books: the *Bible* and the collected laws of the Danish Realm, *Karnovs Lovsamling*. Naturally, what else could an officer of the law possibly need?

I looked out of a window facing the road; it was dead calm outside. Not a soul, not a single vehicle. It was probably too early on a Saturday night for youths partying at the wheel.

The other door from the living room opened into a sizeable kitchen with benches along the walls and a pantry in a corner. Below the windows facing the mountainside was a kitchen counter with its sink and electric stove. I leaned across the stove to get a better look out the window on this side, and felt the heat from one of the hotplates. I touched the kettle on the adjacent burner; it was warm.

Someone had very recently put the kettle on for themselves. Looking around I noticed a mug on the dining table in the corner. I went over and found it half full of tea.

That was when I noticed the crumpled canvas bag on the bench behind the table. I reached for the bag and it rattled when I lifted it onto the table. As I was about to open the bag, I heard the soft creaking of a door, but before I had a chance to turn around something hit me, and I disappeared into pitch-black darkness.

23

'What are ye doing here?'

A voice speaking Suðuroy dialect pierced the dark and the pain. I came to, slowly, swearing under my breath. This wasn't the first time something like this had happened to me.

'Why are ye on the kitchen floor?'

I moaned as searing pain shot through my head. I was about to throw up.

'Who was the bastard that barged into me when I opened the front door?'

The high-pitched voice cut into my head, as if someone was thrusting a knife in.

'Hold on,' I mumbled and hauled myself onto the end of a bench. 'Gimme a minute, please.'

'Give ye a minute!' Now she was pissed off. 'Find ye lying here in pabba's house and, what, ye wannae be left in peace. Answer me now or I'm callin' the police.'

I opened my eyes and looked at the woman standing in the middle of the kitchen floor. She was slim with white permed hair and glittering glasses. Long golden earrings dangled from her earlobes.

'No need to call the police. It's better now,' I said gently to keep the waves of pain from flooding my head. The nausea had already receded a little. As had the vomit in my throat.

'My concern wasnae yer health,' the woman rattled on. 'The hell do ye think I care how ye're bloody doin'? Ye got no sodding business in ma pabba's house.'

'Yes and no,' I replied.

'Don't ye get started ye northern bastard,' the woman pressed on. 'I want a plain answer or I'm reportin' ye.' It was clear from her expression that unless I piped up quickly, this was precisely what was going to happen.

'I came here because Edmund West told me from your father that a canvas bag with something in it was in this basement.'

'Ye know Edmund do ye?' The voice was more obliging now.

'Yes, we're friends.'

'Well, ye could've said so, before I got all in a tiss. Edmund's ma second cousin.' Then she paused. 'But what are ye doin' here? And who was it knocked me over?'

My throat was dry and I asked her for a glass of water. When I'd drained it, I told Edmund's second cousin that I'd come for a canvas bag, but that it was gone when I got into the basement. And since I thought the person who took the bag might be upstairs, I'd gone upstairs. And here I was knocked cold.

'So who's the brute that shoved me so hard I fell? It's a bloody miracle I didnae break both ma arms and legs.'

'I don't know, but you must have got a look at him.'

'No, not properly. It was all so sudden. I unlocked the front door, and it was yanked open instantly, and a bloke in a hat came chargin' out, and I was knocked off ma feet.'

'So you don't know what the man looks like?'

'No, sorry. I don't think I'd recognise him. But if I get ma hands on him, I swear to God I'll haul out his guts, wrap 'em 'round his ears and string him up from the nearest lamp post.'

'Sounds delightful,' I said, and was inclined to agree with the woman's graphic notion of punishment. 'He's also made himself a cup of tea,' I added.

The permed woman with the swinging earrings strode over to the table and grabbed the mug. 'If I get ma hands on that soddin' devil, it'll not be pretty. He'll pine for the tortures of Satan just to get away from me.'

I sat in silent fascination at the older woman's vivid language. She carried on for a good while, and I was starting to agree with the bloke from Suðuroy who once said that youse folks up north, ye swear. Not us, here it's an art.

'Oh Christ,' the woman said suddenly, 'I forgot all about ye. How're ye doin'? Let me take a look at yer neck.'

She touched the back of my head and searing agony shot through me.

'That's where he whacked ye. You've a hole, but a little one. That'll right itself.'

She bent down and picked a rolling pin off the floor. 'This'll be what he bludgeoned ye with.' She weighed the rolling pin in her hand. 'It's a good job he didnae crack yer skull.'

She headed into the living room and moments later returned via the corridor, 'It doesnae look like he's touched anythin' in there. But how come he's been dawdlin' here sipping decades-old tea?'

'I don't know, but my guess is that once he found the canvas bag, he came up here to wait for the ferry back north, to make sure as few people as possible saw him. I just presume that he came south this morning and was planning to head back north on the half six ferry this evening. But then I come along and ruin his plans. He can't get out through the basement, and up here the door is locked with a key. Of course, he could've tried climbing out a window, but then there was a risk the neighbours might notice this odd behaviour, and that I'd hear it. And so he stayed put while I was in the basement, and when I came upstairs, he hid in the pantry.'

'What's in that bag ye're talkin' about? I suppose the stranger made off with it.'

I was briefly torn between telling her and the need to make sure as few people as possible knew about the arm. But it was probably best to keep it under wraps. That way it might be easier to find out who was involved and who wasn't. So I replied that I was on an errand for the police, and unfortunately I wasn't at liberty to tell her.

'Oh aye, just like ma pabba,' she smiled. 'He'd always say that, when there was something us kiddies weren't allowed to know.'

She was clearly used to this and so didn't insist on any further explanation, but I had one more question for her: 'How come you knew we were in your father's house?'

'The woman next door saw ye pull up here and go into the basement, and when ye didnae come back out, she thought it peculiar and phoned me. So I rushed over and looked 'round the basement, but there was no-one there, and then I let maself in up here. The key's on a nail by the door.'

I smiled at this woman, who was all jovial now, while thinking that she may well have saved my life. Had she not arrived in that precise instant, there was no telling what the man hiding in the pantry would have done.

24

Sunday noon I was in the car on my way to Sumba. I would have liked to head south early in the day, but it wasn't done to visit people either before or during Sunday service. So I'd waited until it neared twelve before setting course for the southernmost village in the Faroes. And, according to the villagers themselves, where the true giants lived.

I'd spent the night at Hotel Tvøroyri, and I couldn't fault the experience. Except for my impatience to keep digging and figure out what was going on. Edmund's second cousin had invited me to hers, but my head ached and I really wasn't up to chit-chatting into the small hours, so I'd thanked her, but checked into the hotel instead. I ordered fish and chips for dinner and a coke to go with it. I was thirsty for something stronger, but I didn't know if I had concussion, so best to abstain. At the hotel I got two painkillers, and they made a world of difference. It wasn't even eleven by the time I fell asleep. That meant I was awake by seven in the morning, had my breakfast and had then been wandering around the village trying to pass the time.

Not much happened on a Sunday morning in Tvøroyri, and once I'd been back and forth through a long stretch of the village twice and down to the harbour thrice and only crossed paths with a few roaming dogs, I returned to my room and lay down on the bed to wait.

I tried to think, but I was missing too many pieces to fit together, and all the while the radio was blasting a singing congregation at such volume that it felt as if I was sitting on a church pew. Afterwards they broadcast soothing music, and then I was about to doze off, but managed to pull myself off the bed and out the door. When I reached the village of Vágur it struck me that I hadn't had a single smoke since I was on board *Smyril*. Perhaps I would end up quitting without even thinking about it? I certainly didn't feel like a cigarette right at that moment, my head still wasn't a hundred per cent.

In Vágur I saw two young women pushing prams. That was it. Shortly afterwards I drove into the Sumba Tunnel, which, as opposed to the tunnels in Norðoyggjar, had all the latest high specs. Two lanes and lights in the roof.

The sun was blazing as I slowly motored down towards Sumba, a picture of tranquillity in the sunshine. The problem now was finding the blokes who, back in the day, had found the arm bones. Karl hadn't told me who they were.

I drove into a lay-by and phoned Karl on the mobile, he didn't pick up. Then I called the station in Tórshavn and asked after him, but the man who took the call said that Karl wouldn't be in before two. He was still at home. I hesitated briefly, not sure if I dared to call his house in case Katrin should get to the phone first. I wasn't sure that I could face getting a bucket of shit poured over me. I rang anyway, and mercifully it was Karl who answered.

'So you're brave enough to dial this number?' he goaded me. 'What if Katrin had picked up, you'd never have made it through alive.'

'But she didn't pick up, did she?' I replied.

'Not, but only because she went for a walk up to Hvítanes with the girls in the sunshine. I'm neck-deep in work, so I couldn't go.'

'Yeah, you drew the long straw. You wriggled out of it,' I laughed.

'That's one way of putting it,' Karl returned the laughter, but then grew serious.

'Bergur told you about the man they found in your car in the Árnafjarðar Tunnel.'

'He did, yes. Do you know who he is?'

'No, not yet, but I reckon it won't be long until we find out. I've also sent two officers north to search the cave at Á Gjáum this afternoon when the currents are weak at the turn of the tide. Hopefully they'll make it in.'

Then I told Karl that I was in Suðuroy, and that he'd get the whole story as soon as I got back, but for now I needed him to tell me who the men were who'd found the arm. Once he'd told me and insisted that he wanted to know how it went, we cut the call.

A twinge of guilt reminded me that I hadn't told him about the canvas bag, which I had nearly had my hands on, or that I was knocked cold. But everything was plenty complicated as it was, and I couldn't predict how things would play out if Karl knew. All I wanted right now was a free hand to investigate, and though it was true that Karl had asked me to look into this, it wasn't necessary to tell him *everything*. At least not yet.

In reality I didn't quite know why I'd come to Sumba, because I didn't expect to be told much. It was probably a mix of being here in the south anyway, and disappointment that the canvas bag had slipped through my fingers. And it wasn't entirely inconceivable that something could come of the trip.

I stopped the car outside a tall white concrete house, which Karl had identified as the home of the man with the two sons. I knocked and a girl of around ten opened the door.

I asked her after the man Karl had mentioned, but she just looked up at me and then turned around and shouted: 'Pabba, there's a northerner askin' after granddad.'

A man dressed in a white shirt, black tie and dark trousers came to the door. His clothes told me he'd been to church.

'Yer looking for ma father?' said the man, who was somewhere in his mid-forties. He was broad-shouldered, but his face was lean. A labourer.

'Yes, Karl Olsen, Detective Superintendent at the Criminal Investigation Department in Tórshavn, said that your father many years ago found the bones of an arm.'

'Aye, so he did, and I with him. It was at the foot of Beinisvørð. But come on into the front room.'

I followed the man, and as we passed the kitchen the smell of roast lamb made my mouth water.

The girl trailed us into the front room, but the father asked her to leave, this wasn't for kiddies. She clearly intended to protest, but the father shot her a look, and she left.

This front room was not much different from that of the old policeman in Trongisvágur, and there were as many photos on display. On one wall hung a large painting of the islet Sumbiarhólmur in heavy surf.

The man followed my gaze and said, 'William Smith painted that one. In my view the finest painter in the Faroes. But that's not what youse northerners think.'

I let the last comment slide, but agreed with him that this was a terrific painting.

'Youse don't have that kind of weather north on the mainland. In our village ye certainly cannae walk around in slippers all yer days,' he scoffed.

This too I let slide, and asked after his father.

'No, he died in 1998, and that's when the wife and I moved in here with ma momma. She passed in 2005.'

'I believe one of your brothers was also with you out to Beinisvørð that day?' I said.

'Aye, but he later moved to Denmark, Hirtshals, where he's now both a captain and shipowner. Maself I fish these shores. Someone has to keep the village goin.' 'By the sound of him the entirety of Sumba's future rested on his shoulders.

I made a mental note to try to get my questions answered before I got hopelessly entangled in the southern bravado.

'How were the bones lying when you found them?'

It was as if the man had been away in another world and woke up with my question, 'Oh, the bones, aye.' He thought for a moment and then said, 'There'd been a rockslide on Beinisvørð shortly before, and ma brother and I joined father west to check the damage. We'd heard that a fair few guillemot ledges had been lost, right where we used to go fowlin.' The rockslide was titanic, one of the biggest in Faroese history. Quite possibly the biggest.' He eyed me to see if I would protest.

I was not about to.

'We sailed right up to all the rocks, and they were peppered with dead birds. Then suddenly ma brother spotted somethin' and yelled that a few fathoms ahead lay an arm. We sailed closer, and there lay the arm with an iron shackle round its wrist and the stump of a chain.'

'Were the bones in a heap?'

'No, they were lyin' the way they're built inside your arm. I cannae say if a finger tip may have been out of joint, but other than that.' He looked at me.

'It sounds very peculiar,' I said.

'We all agreed 'bout that. When we tried to lift the arm the bones scattered and we put them in a plastic bag we had on board. How the arm came to be in perfect shape all the way down by the shore after a rockslide like that is impossible to know. Perhaps the hidden *huldufolk* were at play?'

To keep things cordial I agreed and said that there was much between heaven and earth unknown to man. The man wholeheartedly concurred with me on that count.

'You didn't find any more of the skeleton?' I continued.

'No, but the bones could have been there somewhere in all the debris. We just took those bones and didnae go ashore. Pebbles and rocks kept tumblin' down, and we didnae know if there'd be another slide. It was too dangerous to be near, so we sailed away again. In any case we didnae see any more bones,' he added finally.

'When you came back to Sumba, you took the bones to the church?'

'When we got back to the village, we pulled the boat up and began thinkin' what best to do with the bones. Father didnae think we could leave human bones stuffed in a plastic bag, and that the bones may well be of a Christian man. Though the shackle on the wrist might be a sign that these were Turks or some such thing. No matter, we headed up to the church with the bones and on the altar we pieced them together as best we could. I think we did rather well. The only bit we couldnae find was the very tip of the left little finger. Later Kalurin, and that fellow who's now superintendent at the Criminal department, drove south and left with the lot.'

'He told me you wound up having quite the merry night at yours.'

'Oh, aye, father hadnae long before been shipped a crate of beer, and we started chattin' about where such an arm could've come from. When the talk takes an eerie turn a soothin' little nip does a world o' good.' His expression grew animated.

I thought to myself that a beer would do me good right now, but it was doubtful that this Sumba man had a drop on a Sunday.

As if he'd read my thoughts he said, looking serious now: 'Personally I found Jesus when I met ma wife, and havnae touched the drink since.'

So much for that beer, I thought, and asked: 'Didn't you all agree that the arm was probably from one of the *Westerbeek* crew?'

'Aye, we did, and later, when ma father and I and ma brother would sometimes talk about it, we all agreed that the arm was off the Dutch ship. Some poor soul must have been chained on board when the ship ran ashore, and there wouldnae have been any savin' him.'

I drew my own conclusions, but said nothing. Merely bid him farewell and thanked him for his hospitality. Better leg it before I was invited to Sunday dinner at a teetotaller's with a pious wife.

25

Smyril anchored in Tórshavn at about half seven Sunday evening. My trip south hadn't yielded the results I'd hoped for. I'd envisaged returning to Tórshavn with a canvas bag with the bones of an arm in it. And placing it on the table in front of a stunned Detective Superintendent. One Karl Olsen. Instead, I returned empty-handed. I didn't know the present whereabouts of the bag, but I suspected that it and the bones it carried now lay on the bottom of the Atlantic somewhere between Tvøroyri and Tórshavn.

When I got home, I opened a beer and plonked myself down in the living room and put old Leonard Cohen on the record player. The LP was from my first years as a student in Århus, and it was scratched, but all the crackling just brought out the right melancholy mood. I felt pretty alone in the world. My ex was angry and in Copenhagen with my daughter, my oldest friend was willing to talk to me again, but his wife was furious, and another friend was lying in a hospital bed. A stranger had tried to kill me in Norðoyggjar, and in Suðuroy I'd been knocked out. Didn't have a woman either. The line 'Weary the warrior in deserted hall…' by poet Janus Djurhuus came to me, as Leonard Cohen crooned about 'Suzanne'.

Janus I brushed off, though. No need to wallow, and then I remembered that Haraldur and Sanna were back. And Judith, who I'd also just talked to. Everything seemed to brighten a little, and my thoughts turned to considering my next steps.

Perhaps I could call Judith and ask if she wanted to have dinner with me at a restaurant. It wasn't yet nine o'clock.

The mobile phone rang a few times before Judith answered, and when I'd asked, she replied that she was at work, and on a double shift, that she wasn't off work until seven the next morning. I was just about to ask if I could take her out another day, when she said the alarm had gone off in one of the rooms and that she had to hang up.

I felt a little sheepish, sitting there with the phone to my ear. On the other hand, she hadn't said that she didn't want to dine with me, she just couldn't tonight.

I went into the kitchen to check what was in the fridge. Nothing much. Cheese and liver pate and a bag of rye bread. That was when I heard something from the hall, and when I got there I noticed a vibrating sound from my jacket. It was the mobile. Before I could answer it went quiet. When I pulled it out, I saw a missed call from Karl. He'd called fifteen minutes ago too, but I hadn't noticed because my phone was out here, and because I didn't know the ringtone. That's what it's like to get a new phone. I returned his call.

'Where are you, Hannis? Why don't you answer when people call?' were his first words.

'I'm home, and if you'd called on the landline, I would've picked up. The mobile was in my jacket, which was hanging in the entrance.'

'That's just like you,' Karl scoffed. 'Hardly a tech whizz.'

'Well, I've never claimed to be one. But I don't suppose you're phoning on a Sunday evening to tell me that.'

'Sunday evening!' Karl spluttered. 'What does it matter that it's Sunday evening? When people are getting murdered you work until the cases are solved.'

'Yeah, well, I'm not in the force, as you've so often repeated.'

This shut him up, for a split second: 'Oh, don't know about that, the way you've meddled in all manner of ways for years you'd think you belonged here. And when for once you're asked to lend us a hand, no, then *monsieur* doesn't work down at the station.' The last bit was said in a mocking tone.

'It wasn't meant like that, I just meant...'

'Who cares what you meant. The question is whether you're working with us on this case or not?'

'I'm happy to work with the police.'

'And tell us everything?'

'Yes.'

'Even about visiting a house where someone who served as an officer in Tvøroyri together with Kalurin once lived?'

My ears turned crimson. 'It wasn't because I wanted to hide anything from you,' I protested. 'It was just easier to tell you about it in person.'

'And when were you planning for us to meet?'

'I don't know,' I replied hesitatingly. 'Tonight maybe?'

'Yes, precisely. Tonight. Get yourself over here as soon as, you'll get to tell your story, and then I have another to tell you.'

I assumed it was about the dead man in the tunnel, and that could wait. Instead I asked,

'But how did you know that I'd been to that house in Tvøroyri?'

'The old officer's daughter wasn't born yesterday, she called the police down south and told them about the incident. They then phoned us here at the central station, but they didn't know the identity of the man the woman had found knocked out on the kitchen floor. I, however, could put two and two together. I knew you were in Suðuroy, so it could hardly be anyone else.'

'Don't know about that…' I tried to protest.

'The lady had also told them that you'd said that you'd come for a canvas bag, but that the contents were secret and that's why you couldn't tell her anything about that. Am I relaying what transpired correctly?'

'Yes,' I replied, on tenterhooks.

'But that a man ran off with the bag.'

'Yes.'

There was a silence on the line for a moment, then Karl muttered quietly: 'Just come on over, then we'll talk about it.'

He hung up.

It was when Karl went all mild that he was at his most ter-rifying, so I grabbed my coat and hurried out the door.

26

It was after midnight by now, and Karl and I were still in his office. When I first came over he'd been a little testy, but once he'd heard what happened to me in Suðuroy he forgot to sulk and started interrogating me instead. How could the man who knocked me cold in Trongisvágur know that the bag of bones was in precisely that basement? No-one but the old officer, Edmund West, and I knew that.

I had no answer.

It was clear to him that if we linked this to the bloke who assaulted me up north, then Edmund played a pivotal role. But at the same time it made no sense. All Edmund had done was talk to a cousin of his dad's who in turn happened to have the canvas bag with the bones. Then he'd told me about it, and I hadn't told a soul.

I also told Karl that someone had tried to make their way into Edmund's room on Friday night during my late visit. And that the nurses had been called away, so they weren't on the ward.

'There's something going on at the hospital which we're missing,' Karl eventually concluded.

'What is it?' I asked.

'I don't know, but that's what my detective gut is telling me.'

This was where my part of the story was put on hold while Karl's took over.

They'd tried to identify the bloke who ten years ago was a fair-haired young man, and who, after he'd had a few, paid the station a visit on Ólavsøka. And they had succeeded, Kunoy wasn't that big a village after all, but he was away at sea.

His family, only the one sister, heard from him every once in a while. She said that she thought he was living in San Francisco, and that he worked as a radio operator on a tanker. That's all she knew.

'It would appear this bloke is hiding too,' Karl said. But then added, 'He might also just have gone to sea. Seeing a skeleton deep in a seal cave in his youth might not be at the forefront of his mind. Except perhaps in dreams.'

He stared into space for a moment and then went on to tell me who the little man in the beret was. His name had been Áki Hansen and he grew up in Tórshavn. He'd lived in Denmark for many years, partly in Aarhus, and Karl wanted to know if I'd heard of him in my time in Denmark. I hadn't. The cops in Denmark did, however, know Åge Hansen, as they called him, very well indeed. So well, in fact, that he'd spent more than half of the last twenty-odd years lodged at their expense. He'd dabbled in all sorts. Pimping, credit card fraud, conning people by renting out apartments he didn't own, and he didn't shy away from violence if need be. For a pocket-sized man he was a very skilled fighter, and had no qualms about using knives. Rumours in Aarhus had it that he'd allegedly killed more than one person, but the police had never been able to prove it. In short, a nasty little rat, Karl concluded.

I asked how he could know the grotto at Á Gjáum if he was from Tórshavn. Karl explained that Áki Hansen grew up in Tórshavn, but his mum was from Kunoy and he'd often holidayed there.

Karl and I agreed that Ísak Joensen and Áki Hansen had returned to the Faroe Islands and turned up murdered shortly after. We knew that much.

'Maybe it was Áki Hansen who killed Ísak Joensen,' I mused.

'Perhaps,' Karl replied, 'but why? How did he know that Ísak had returned to his home village? Áki returned two days after Ísak did.'

'Someone sent for him?' I suggested.

'Not unthinkable, but who? And who killed Áki?'

'Haven't the foggiest, but he was a crafty bugger. I mean, when I met him he was wearing a beret, patterned jumper and gumboots. I mean, the man just landed from Denmark after decades abroad, and looks exactly like your average bloke in Klaksvík.'

'You can't be a career criminal without picking up a few tricks,' Karl said. 'He couldn't just rock up in Klaksvík dressed like someone straight off a Danish city street. He had to blend in, and he knew how.'

Karl stood up and started pacing. 'All we've got are questions, hardly any answers. Not just about these two, but also the canvas bag.'

Silence reigned in the office. Only punctuated by footsteps and voices from the corridor, and then the traffic from the road.

Karl broke the silence. 'I've got something I want to tell you, something I've been suspecting, but now think I've confirmed. But you mustn't breathe a word about it to anyone. Not a word.' He fixed me with his eyes and sat back down.

I promised.

'We managed to get into the cave up north today and to extract the skeleton. They also managed to spend the best part of an hour searching the location, but found no further evidence. Apart from the skeleton and fragments of clothes, that is,' Karl added.

'I've seen the skeleton,' I said. 'It can't have been pleasant for him sitting there alone in the dark waiting for death.'

'You're right about that,' Karl said. 'But why are you saying *him*?'

The question took me aback and I hesitated, 'Well, I just sort of figured…' It slowly dawned on me. 'Are you saying you found the remains of a woman?'

'Correct, and we know who she is too.'

'Blimey,' I said with admiration. 'How did you manage that?'

'Did you spot a cap in the cave?'

'What was left of one, yeah.'

'The woman's name was in it. *Maud Simonsen*.'

'Who was she?'

'A fish factory worker in her mid-twenties who disappeared in the second half of the 1950s. People just assumed she'd left the country. She hadn't, she was chained in a cave in northern Kunoy.'

'You're certain it's her?'

'It's a female skeleton, and then there's the name. That'll do for now. And I'm being told that she was renowned during the Klaksvík Revolt for knocking the feathered hat off the Danish High Commissioner.'

'It was hardly the Danish authorities that killed her.'

'Nah, that's not my working theory either,' Karl smiled. 'But in the olden days a stunt like that would have landed you in a ball and chain. I wonder if she wasn't jailed for a couple of days for it,' Karl pondered.

'So, is this what I'm not supposed to let anyone in on?' I asked, a bit baffled.

'What?' Karl said, snapping back into focus. 'Don't be daft, that thing about the High Commissioner is common knowledge. At least in Klaksvík. No, what I wanted to tell you is that when Ísak Joensen's body was autopsied, it was found that he was missing the tip of the little finger on his left hand, and that it had been missing for many years.'

'The bloke in Sumba told me,' I interrupted, 'that the only bone missing to complete the arm was the outer tip of the little finger, or *last finger*, as they call it down south. He just supposed it'd been lost.'

'You don't say,' Karl muttered, 'I suspected as much.'

'How could you suspect it?' I asked, perplexed. 'Just because Ísak Joensen's skeleton was missing that joint, it doesn't…' I shut my mouth as it sank in. 'Maud Simonsen's skeleton was also one little finger joint short?'

'It was indeed. It wasn't until today that I surmised there may be something to this. When the two colleagues brought the skeleton back this afternoon and it was pieced together at the hospital, it puzzled me that all the bones were accounted for except precisely this one. I asked them if they'd searched the sandy ground in the cave well enough. They swore they did, and if that joint existed, it wasn't on that sand bank. That's when it started to feel like an odd coincidence. We find a man shackled last week and a woman shackled years ago. Both missing the tip of their left little finger. And now you come and tell me that the bloke from Sumba told you that the very same joint was missing from the arm found beneath Beinisvørð. And the arms were all shackled too. There's evidently a connection, but we just don't know enough yet to see what's behind it.'

'When you were in Sumba back then with Kalurin to pick up the arm bones, you didn't notice this joint missing?'

'Not at all. There were some bones on the altar and they'd been laid out so there was an arm with a hand and fingers. But whether every joint was accounted for, I didn't notice.'

'So you trust that the Sumba man is telling the truth?'

'Why wouldn't he be telling the truth? Because he's gone off the drink?' Karl smiled. 'Besides, it matches the other two skeletons we have perfectly. The arm found in Sumba didn't come from the *Westerbeek*, but more likely belonged to some-one from Klaksvík.'

'How d'you know that?' I quizzed Karl.

'The deceased up north were both from Klaksvík, and the little finger on the arm down south is also missing this joint. The logical conclusion is that there's at least a ninety-percent likelihood that its owner was from Klaksvík.'

'Ok, that doesn't sound too far-fetched. Just makes it even more bloody unfortunate that someone swiped the canvas bag from under our noses.'

'Very, and seeing as it slipped right through your butterfin-gers, I also expect you to go back to Suðuroy and attempt to remedy your mistake.'

I started to say, 'I didn't make any mis…', but Karl cut me off.

'You're going back south tomorrow to ask around after a northerner from Klaksvík who may have gone missing on the island sometime between the mid-1950s and approximately 1960.'

'Why am I getting caught up in this? You detectives are much better at answering questions like that than I am.'

'I've already searched our records for any missing people down south from the previous century until the Beinisvørð rockslide. Sure, there were a few, but no one fitting our context. No, you're going south, and all you have to do is find out whether a northerner from Klaksvík went missing within a five-year timespan. That should be feasible for a hard-nosed journalist.'

'And if I don't go?'

'Then we'll be cutting off the hot water. You won't be getting any info, and you won't be getting anywhere near anything remotely related to police matters. You won't be taking a single step without one of us laying snares for you.'

'All right, message received. But what's in it for me if I do go south?'

'Well, you might, for example, find yourself invited to dinner with Katrin and yours truly at our place up in Stoffalág.'

'You can't make me!' I blurted out, 'When it comes to women, I agree with Shakespeare: "Hell hath no fury like a woman scorned." And it makes not the slightest difference if it's on her friend's behalf.'

The detective superintendent flashed a satisfied grin.

27

Karl had told me that *Smyril* would weigh anchor from Tórshavn Monday morning at half eight, so he surmised that I had plenty of time for some shuteye. It was two in the morning, but I didn't much feel like going straight home and it occurred to me that Lágargarður wasn't far.

The front door was locked, and I was about to get back in the car and leave, but then I mustered the courage to ring Judith Christiansen's mobile. She answered almost straight away and when I told her I was at the entrance, she said she would come out and let me in.

A heartbeat later the door opened and Judith invited me inside. We walked along the corridor in silence, turned into the dining room and closed the door.

'This is a very late visit,' Judith said with a serious expression.

'I was down at the station, and since I knew you would be on shift until tomorrow morning, I thought I'd stop by.'

'Perhaps you're attending to some business,' she asked, looking just as grave.

'Oh, I don't know about business. But I wanted to talk to you. Ever since you called this spring, I've been feeling guilty about being so abrupt. Then when you approached me in SMS, I got the impression that it was possible for us to talk to each other, that we didn't necessarily have to be on bad terms.'

Judith took my hand and I could see the smile in her eyes.

'Hannis, love, I don't hold a grudge against you. It just became a bit of a mess. Neither of us is at fault really, other than for both deciding to go home together, and then chance played a trick on us.'

'That's good to hear,' I said, and the constant feeling I'd had of being both embarrassed and a little guilty lifted. At the same time, this conversation was making me feel a bit uncomfortable. Talking about emotions wasn't my strong suit.

'You wouldn't happen to have a cup of coffee?' I asked in the end, just to stop dwelling on this.

'Of course, have a seat, and I'll get you coffee. Would you like a bite too?'

That was when I noticed how hungry I was. I hadn't eaten anything since some time in the afternoon, I'd forgotten all about food in Karl's office.

'If you have some, I'd love a slice of bread. I've hardly eaten today.'

'I've got frozen lasagne. I'll pop it in the microwave, it'll be ready in a couple of minutes. I made it myself,' she added with a smile.

'That would be brilliant.'

'You can have a glass of red too, if you'd like. One of the residents turned ninety-five today, and I think there's half a bottle of wine under the table here somewhere.'

'No, lasagne and coffee are perfect. I'm catching *Smyril* tomorrow morning, so best to abstain.'

'As you please,' said Judith, who seemed more beautiful to me than ever.

While I ate we talked about this and that and afterwards we took the coffee with us out on a bench facing east. There we wrapped up and watched the sunrise. It was a magnificent fiery display of hues from magenta via orange to shimmering bright yellow. The islands looked like they were on fire.

When I later drove home, I was certain that it wouldn't be long before I saw Judith again.

28

I dozed in one of the aviator chairs all the way south and soaked up none of nature's glory this summer day. I had done both yesterday and the day before, though, and that would have to suffice. When *Smyril* docked I woke up feeling better than when I boarded the ferry. The nap meant I'd slept a total of four hours in the last twenty-four, and that was more than enough for real men. At least that's what they claimed in the southernmost village of the Faroes, where I was headed.

You could hardly call Sumba busy this Monday morning. After sitting in the car in the middle of the village for fifteen minutes, I still hadn't seen a soul. Not even a dog. So I got out intending to knock on a door somewhere to enquire, but first I strolled out to the landing place. It was usually a place where you would find people.

A middle-aged man in yellow overalls and a chequered flat cap was painting a big white inshore boat. I approached him and said good morning.

He stood up, stretched his back and replied: 'Northerner?'

It was as much a declaration as it was a question.

'That's right, from Tórshavn,' I said. 'Mind if I ask you about some…'

'Were ye in the village the day before yesterday?' the man asked abruptly. He hadn't shaved for a couple of days, his dark stubble was long.

'Yes, I was here on Saturday, but that…'

'Ye with the police?'

I was going to say no, but it wouldn't be easy to get any answers out of this bloke, so perhaps a little authority might help.

'Yes, I'm from the police in Tórshavn.'

'Aye right, well, then I've naethin' to say,' said the man and bent back down to carry on painting.

I was taken aback, but said, 'You have to answer questions from the police.'

'Not unless ye drag me to court.' He dipped the brush in the paint pot and stroked the boards.

'Yes, but…' I was at a loss.

'That arsehole of a copper in Tvøroyri slapped a fine on me last year. He's a northerner,' he said, looking at me as if that was sufficient explanation. 'That flamin' bastard claimed I was fishing with too fine a mesh.'

'Even so, you could still answer a question for me.'

'No, I promised there and then that if the cops ever wanted anythin' of me again, they'd have to drag me before a judge. I wonnae be bloody volunteering.' He resumed painting.

It was clear to me that I wouldn't be getting anything out of this guy, and a bit late now to admit that I wasn't part of the force. So I turned up the hill and walked back to the car.

Not far from the car I met a smiling woman in a white dress with bold red floral print. 'Did ye have a chat with the grump down at the landin'?'

'I tried, but when he heard I was with the police, he refused to talk to me. Said that I'd have to drag him before a judge, if I wanted anything out of him.'

'Sounds about right,' the woman laughed. 'He's an oddball of an old bachelor, and since he was fined for his meshes he's barely spoken of anythin' else.'

'Might you perhaps be able to help me instead?' I asked politely.

'Who knows?' she said and her smile broadened.

'I'm looking for someone from Klaksvík who lived here in the south in the late 1950s.'

'Sweetheart, no, how old d'ye think I am?' she teased me. 'But, ye know what, if ye come home with me, ma momma will be in. She might know.'

140

I thanked her for the invitation and headed further into the village with the cheery woman.

When we entered the kitchen there was an older lady at the stove frying fishcakes. She turned to me with a smile and said good day, and in the same movement she showed me that her hands were dirty, so she couldn't shake my hand. She was somewhere in her mid-seventies with thick glasses, and otherwise seemed to possess the same sunny disposition as her daughter.

'This man is from the police and he's asking if we know about someone from Klaksvík, who's meant to have lived 'round here in the late 1950s.'

The older lady dropped the last fishcake in the pan, rinsed her hands under the tap and then replied: 'There were several northerners in the village of Lopra back in the 1950s. I grew up in Lopra maself, I remember many who came south to work at the whaling station stayin' on.'

'This person wouldn't have arrived until about 1955.'

'Bear with me, I'll try to think back.' She smiled and turned to flip the fishcakes in the frying pan.

'This is a long time back,' she said after a while. 'But I remember someone they said was from Klaksvík. I was twenty then, workin' at the shop. A northerner used to come in, always just before closin'. Sometimes we'd already turned the key when he knocked at the door.'

'Do you recall his name?'

'Not right now, but it might come.' She lifted the lid of a pot with simmering potatoes and pierced them with a sharp knife. 'Five more minutes and they're done.'

The daughter set the table and asked if I wouldn't join them for lunch. 'There's plenty, and it's only the two of us and the kiddies.'

I asked after the husband and was told that he was in the merchant marine, a Mærsk officer, and wouldn't be back for another month.

There was a clatter from the stairs and a girl and a boy tumbled into the kitchen. They stopped in their tracks when they saw me.

'Ye better behave now,' the grandmother said, 'that man's a police officer from Tórshavn, and God help us if he sees how ye mites muck about.'

The children, a girl of about eleven and a boy of about nine, stood there staring at me for a while, then the boy said: 'D'ye have a gun?'

'No, I left it in Tórshavn.'

'How d'ye plan on shootin' anyone then?'

'I'm not planning on shooting anyone.'

'I thought that's what the cops did,' said the boy.

'That's just in films, here in the Faroes we don't shoot anyone.'

'When I grow up I'm gonna be a policeman. Not here in the Faroes, there aren't any real criminals here, but maybe in New York.'

I thought to myself, little do you know, kiddo, about what goes on in these isles. All the while the daughter was telling her mum about a girl who was so mean and had torn the collar off her dress. The mother comforted her, promising to sew the collar back on.

The kids wolfed down lunch, said thanks and disappeared back out the door. It made me think of Turið and how much I missed her. I should call her.

When coffee and biscuits were on the table, the grandmother recounted that she'd heard people say that this northerner had been involved in the Klaksvík Revolt, but that he'd fled south. She also recalled that people found it a little odd that he'd left Klaksvík, because he was part of the majority, the so-called Ninety-Fivers. She didn't know what a Ninety-Fiver was at the time and had asked. They'd told her that during the Klaksvík Revolt ninety-five percent of the villagers had signed a petition, and that was how they got the name.

'Yes, and the others, who disagreed and didn't sign, they were branded Fivers,' I said.

'I learned that later, but it was still peculiar how frightened this man was. It was very clear he was hiding from someone, and sometimes he'd ask us if anyone from Klaksvík had asked after him. That's also why he did his shopping so late. Because it was dark by then, and nobody would see him.'

'Which time of year was this?' I asked.

'Would've been right before Christmas, we had these sheets of cut-out Christmas elves for sale. I asked him one time, if he wasnae gunna decorate for Christmas and showed him a sheet, but he just scoffed saying he didnae have time for that kind of twaddle.'

'Do you know where he was living?'

'There was a house up in the fields, practically a summer cottage. He was renting it.'

'How long did he live there?'

'A few months, I remember talking about it, and it would've been 'round Shrove Tuesday, that he hadnae been to the shop for near two weeks. We never saw him again.'

'Do you recall any more about him? What he looked like?'

'He wasnae very tall, but had big hands. Oh, and now I remember,' said the affable grandmother, 'he was missin' the tip of his left last finger.'

'Bingo,' I thought.

'I asked him how he lost it, and he said he'd been guttin' fish on a ship deck when the knife slipped.'

She fell silent, and the daughter said she'd never heard of that bloke from Klaksvík. The grandmother said she'd hardly spared him a thought, until she was asked. But when one goes back in time it's like pulling at the end of a ball of yarn, and you just keep unravelling more and more.

'*Emil*,' she blurted out suddenly. 'His name was *Emil*. The last name I cannae recall, doubt I was ever told it.'

I asked if she knew of anyone who perhaps knew something about this Emil, but she said that it was probably her and the other girl in the shop who'd seen him the most. Little as it was. When I asked after the other shop attendant, she said that she'd moved to Norway years ago and was married in Tønsberg.

In the end I thanked her and said that she'd been a great help. I also thanked her daughter for the hospitality and was making to leave when the grandmother added: 'What's clearest in ma mind now is how terrified he was. Fear had its hooks in him, and I got the impression he felt his fate was sealed. Like there was naethin' could be done. No matter what, he was doomed.'

29

Back in Tórshavn I dropped in at the station and reported what I had found out to Karl.

'We'll identify that guy, no problem,' Karl said with a satisfied expression on his tired face. 'Can't have been that many Emils in Klaksvík in the mid-1950s.' He poured himself coffee from a thermos and carried on, 'You see, Hannis, sending you south was the right thing to do. Within an hour you sniffed out both a name and that the man was missing the tip of his left little finger. The question now is what exactly this last piece of information means.' He glanced over at me.

'What do I know? It's odd, though.'

'You're saying that this lady told you that this Emil was petrified of something. She didn't know of what?'

'No, no idea, but she said that it was as if he'd lost all hope of escape. He was just waiting for the execution.'

'And it came. There's hardly any doubt that he was chained in a cave beneath Beinisvørð and the rockslide uncovered him.'

'He can't have been sitting deep inside, then the arm would never have seen the light of day,' I theorised.

'We can sit here guessing 'til Judgement Day, but until we get our hands on the perpetrator, we won't know anything for certain.'

'Presuming the perpetrator is alive. It's a long time ago.'

'Well, someone is alive, otherwise Ísak Joensen wouldn't have been drowned and attempts made to murder you and what followed after that.'

'By "what followed" you mean what happened with Áki Hansen and that I was knocked out in Trongisvágur.'

'That's one way of putting it,' Karl smiled and continued: 'Both Ísak Joensen and Áki Hansen are dead, and you were knocked out, so there's a criminal on the loose. And it's him we have to catch as quickly as possible.'

'How?'

'There's the nub, but maybe you could help us?'

'Again? Have you no people?'

'Yeah, we've some people, and they've been working round the clock for days. The head of accounting tells me that we've already clocked up reams of overtime, so staff need to be given time off in lieu of pay. One thing's absolutely certain, we won't be getting any additional financial allocation. Besides, have you anything better to do?'

I had to admit that I didn't, but I still asked: 'What will I get in return for doing the legwork for the police? And spare me that offer of dinner with you and Katrin.'

'I can't promise you an exclusive, but you can be the first to run the story. In addition, you could find yourself on better terms with parts of the force that haven't had such an easy time with you these last months.'

I gave in, and Karl and I spent some time considering how I might go about things. In the end we agreed that I should head north to Klaksvík early the following day and make enquiries amongst the older inhabitants. Someone might know something about the three who departed without the tip of their little fingers.

Karl phoned for sandwiches, and while we ate we discussed whether there might be more skeletons lurking around the country. Whether more people had been shackled in caves or on the foreshore. It was an unnerving thought, but we couldn't rule it out, seeing as we'd discovered two of the skeletons by sheer chance.

30

As I walked up the steps to my house, I noticed that the glass pane in my front door was smashed. I swore and retreated to the front yard to call the police. The officer on duty asked if it was a break-in or vandalism. Whether someone had just tossed a stone through the door? I hadn't thought of that and promised to call back after checking it out. Home break-ins were virtually unheard of, but rocks flung by a passer-by weren't. Still, it was Monday evening, not exactly when drunken hordes tend to drift past. At the back of my mind there was also a little voice reminding me that I'd been assaulted more than once in these last few days, so I was on guard.

I opened the basement door and grabbed a shovel right inside it. Holding it high ready to strike, I crept step by step up the stairs to the front door. It was ajar. So, not just a case of antisocial behaviour.

Briefly I considered ringing the station again, but they would probably just ask more questions, so I might as well carry on. I pushed the door with my foot and stepped inside. The crunch of glass under my soles gave me a start, and I stood stock-still, listening. Not a peep.

On tiptoe I approached the living room door and peered inside. It was chaos. Anything that could possibly be toppled had been pushed over, books were torn from the shelves, records and CDs littered the floor. I didn't go in, but approached the kitchen instead; it was in the same state. There hadn't been much in the fridge, but its meagre contents were now shattered and smeared across the floor, glistening in the evening sun beaming through the windows. Everything in the cupboards now also littered the kitchen, which more than any-thing resembled a beach scattered with flotsam.

I paused and pricked up my ears again, but when I couldn't hear anything I went upstairs. Here too the thug had torn through every nook and cranny, even the mattress in my bed was slashed.

I went back downstairs, set down the shovel and phoned the police. The duty officer told me that they'd send someone over tomorrow to inspect the damage. I wanted them to come immediately, but he maintained that whoever had done it was long gone, so it made no difference. Not to panic, they'd be there tomorrow, were his final words before hanging up.

I lived in a duplex and it occurred to me that the neighbours might have heard something. They were an older couple who retired a few years back. I glanced at my watch, which was ap-proaching eleven. That wasn't late. Not in the Faroes at least.

I rang the doorbell and moments later the wife came out.

'Why hello, wasn't expecting you,' she said, and I could hear the television at full blast in the living room.

'Yes, just knocking to ask if you'd heard anything from my house today?'

'Did we hear anything? Good God, yes, all sorts. We were trying to listen to a programme about Elvis Presley on the ra-dio, but there was such a racket coming from yours that we gave up and went over to SMS instead. They've a special offer at the moment on coffee with Danish pastries,' she added.

'What time was this racket?'

'The programme about Elvis was on at three, I remember that, so it must've been about then. D'you know,' my neigh-bour said, and a youthful expression came over her face, 'when I was younger I used to absolutely adore Elvis. I mean, I still love him. He's just in another league compared to this modern noise the radio keeps putting on.'

The unwelcome guest had visited my home mid-afternoon, while I was in Suðuroy.

'Are you knocking walls down?' the woman asked, curiosity beaming from the pale eyes behind glasses. 'My husband said you'd think you were smashing the place to smithereens.'

I silently agreed with the husband and told her that I'd had a break-in, and that the burglar had smashed everything he could lay his hands on.

'Jesus!' the woman exclaimed in horror and stared after me as I walked down the steps. She shouted something about remembering to lock the front door, but I pretended not to hear and went back to mine.

I headed for the living room to examine it closer and I saw that all the paintings on the wall were slashed from one corner to the other. Including the large canvas of a pilot whale hunt by Mikines. My belongings had been trashed indiscriminately for the sheer sake of destruction, and I now noticed that the screen on my computer, which was on the desk by the window, was shattered. There'd been no holding back.

I was automatically about to start tidying, but then I remembered the police. They would have to see this. Not because I thought they would be able to find anyone to arrest, but for the insurance. If I wanted it to cover any of this, then everything would have to be documented and verified by the police. I made a mental note to call my insurance tomorrow, before driving to Klaksvík.

In the basement I found a sheet of plywood that roughly fit the front door, and I nailed it over the broken pane. It kept the worst of the draught out.

There wasn't much else to do apart from go to bed. The slashed mattress could probably be turned over, so I could use it tonight. On the way up I checked the kitchen, in case there was anything to put back in the fridge.

That was when I spotted the footprint. In the flour on the floor there was a footprint with a pattern identical to the one I'd seen in the stable in Trongisvágur.

31

Driving north in the car, Haraldur told me about his time in the Mediterranean. It had been so blasted hot, especially in Rhodes, that he swore that any locals who found themselves sent to hell would be coming back for blankets to keep warm. Haraldur had liked Rome where they'd also made a stop and, seeing as I'd spent several stints living there, we chatted about places we'd visited. We both enjoyed the Palatine Hill inside Forum Romanum, because you could sit in peace and quiet there almost isolated from the cacophony of Rome traffic. Haraldur told me that on their first night they'd had a room facing one of the main roads near the Forum. The din from the cars and scooters had driven him to the bathtub for sleep. The surface was perhaps a little on the hard side, but at least it was quiet.

Somewhere at the back of my mind I was aware that the man who knocked me out in Trongisvágur and the one who broke in were likely to be the same person. The footprint confirmed this and made my unease more tangible, and amplified it. I no longer thought it safe for me to tour the country on my own. So I'd called Haraldur early this morning to ask if he'd come with me to Klaksvík. He replied that he was planning to head out in the boat in the fair weather; he hadn't done any fishing all the time he'd been away. I told him, in a nutshell, what had happened to me, and that I needed someone solid by my side. He replied that, given the circumstances, the fish could wait and I should just come and pick him up in the car.

We'd had balmy weather for over a week now and around the country they were, according to the radio, starting to talk about water scarcity. The meteorologists said that a low-pressure system west of Iceland wasn't moving and neither was a high-pressure system south of the Faroes. For as long as these two stayed put, the weather wouldn't change. Perhaps another week, they wouldn't risk forecasting any further ahead.

Haraldur wasn't from Klaksvík, but from another village up north where you would say '*noy*' for no and tend towards a nasal drawl on every 'á'. It wasn't always easy for people from Tórshavn to establish a rapport with the good folk of Klaksvík, who felt they had every reason to be wary of emissaries of the authorities in the capital. At the end of the day, wasn't that what everyone in Tórshavn was? It wasn't unthinkable that having a true northerner by my side might help clear the steepest hurdles.

The plan was, as Karl had suggested, to contact older people from Klaksvík and see if I could dig anything up about these ill-fated little fingers. I had, in between chats about Rome and the Greek islands, filled Haraldur in on most of what had been going on, and told him that he had to keep this detail about skeletons and missing little finger tips to himself. Only a handful of people knew of them, and we should preferably have arrested whoever was behind the killings before it leaked. Both because it would cause frantic speculation, and because precisely this knowledge could help to make sure we arrested the right person.

We parked in front of the library and went in to use a computer. Mine was, of course, smashed, so I hadn't been able to make a list of care homes in Klaksvík. Many of the people active in the 1950s would be in some home now, and, in any case, it was the easiest way to get in touch with several people in this age bracket.

According to Klaksvík Municipality's website, there were four homes for the elderly in town. The biggest was in an annex to the hospital and it had 36 residents, and then there were three smaller ones. We decided to pay a visit to one of the smaller ones first, we figured it would be easier to get talking to people there.

The care home was a stone's throw from the library, so we left the car where it was and walked up to a large white timber house where eleven older people lived. A portly middle-aged woman received us, enquiring whom we were there to visit.

'Nobody specific, really,' I said. 'We'd just like to ask the residents a couple of questions.'

The woman hadn't been particularly welcoming when we arrived, and now her plump face grew very stern. 'And what might these questions be?'

'Oh, just this and that,' I ventured, 'but particularly about the years in the mid-1950s.'

'So about the Doctor Revolt,' she said, looking daggers at me.

'Yes, perhaps in part, but...'

'There have only recently been two television programmes about this, and that's quite enough. I shan't let strangers from Tórshavn come here and confuse frail old people.'

'We simply wanted...'

The woman cut me off: 'Unless you represent the authorities, I suggest you go now and leave us in peace.'

I was about to protest that I did come from the police, but was at the same time certain that this battle-axe would demand proof, which I didn't possess.

We left.

A few steps down from the care home, I noticed that Haraldur was nearly wetting himself laughing.

'What're you laughing at?' I said, a little wounded.

'Well, it's quite the spectacle to behold when journalists trying to do their job get shoved out the door by a harpy.'

'She wasn't easily budged,' I mustered an embarrassed smile.

'No, she was like an island. Weighing about a skippund,' Haraldur hooted. 'Do you feel like trying any more of these smaller care homes, where it's *easier to get talking to people?*'

'No, sod that, we're heading to the hospital care home,' I replied with a chuckle. 'There has to be someone up here in the dark north who can answer our bloody questions.'

But I was starting to doubt that.

32

Norðoya Røktarheim was a bigger and more modern care home, which meant it was easier to get access to the residents. Haraldur and I just walked straight up and into the first room we found. With the curtains drawn it was gloomy inside; I could make out the silhouette of a man in a bed. He looked at least a century old, but I still took hold of his shoulder.

'What, who?' he mumbled. 'Is it my watch now? I'm coming.' He tried to get up, poking two blue-mottled starling legs out from under the duvet. I tried to press him down, but he was like an eel, I could hardly restrain him.

'Haraldur, come help me before he falls out of bed and injures himself.'

Haraldur gently placed his hand on the man's chest and whispered in a northern dialect that the watch was over and he could go to sleep. That calmed the man, and he lay back. He was soon snoring. During the entire incident his eyes had been closed, which cast an eerie air over the whole scene.

'I think we should try another room,' Haraldur whispered. I nodded in agreement and we stepped into the corridor.

The next room was more promising, at least at first. The old woman was sitting in an armchair reading a magazine. This room was furnished like a little front room with dated furniture. Every wall was decked with photos and embroidered scripture of the type *Bless this Home*. The woman smiled as we stepped inside and enquired whom these guests might be.

'We're from Tórshavn, and the police has sent us to ask older people in Klaksvík a couple of questions.'

The smile on the lady's face faded as she asked: 'What kind of questions?' There was an edge to the voice which should have warned me.

'Oh, it's about the time just after the Klaksvík Revolt, when several people moved away from the village.'

'Town,' the woman said.

'What?' I was baffled.

'It's not just you lot down south who have a town. Klaksvík is a town too, not a village.' Her voice was steely.

'I beg your pardon,' I said in a humbler tone and promised myself to mind my words more here in the north. I saw that Haraldur could barely keep a straight face.

'We merely wish to ask if you know of two men and a woman who are missing the tip of their left little finger?' I asked, thinking that I might as well jump straight in.

Her eyes widened and it seemed to me as if she was quivering.

'There may, of course, be several people who are short of this tip, but for now we know of three,' I said, and stopped in my tracks. The old lady was clearly out of sorts. She was shaking from top to toe. The magazine was on the floor and her mouth was gaping, though at first no sound came from it. Then, all of a sudden, the woman let out a howl. It was as if it came from her belly up through her throat, and was blasted at full volume from her mouth. She was in an utter frenzy.

It came as a complete surprise and shocked me. I was about to put my hand over the old lady's mouth, but Haraldur shook his head and pointed to the door. We hurried out and into the next room before anyone had time to arrive. Then we heard running along the corridor and agitated voices in the room next door. The banshee howl quietened and eventually tapered off.

'What d'you two want?' a voice behind us asked. We turned to see who it belonged to. In a wheelchair by the window sat a sunken man, though his face was lively and the blue eyes had a quick-witted spark. I guessed he must be around Haraldur's age.

I tried to think of a reply, but he continued: 'I suspect you've stomped pretty heavily on my neighbour's toes,' he smirked.

Haraldur replied, 'It wasn't on purpose. Hannis said that we were from the authorities in Tórshavn and wanted to ask her a couple of questions about the years following the Klaksvík Revolt.'

The man in the wheelchair started laughing. 'A happy coincidence then, you came to the right lady. She was in the thick of it in those years, and her husband disappeared in 1955 when it was all over. Most people thought he fled the country, but some claimed he'd been killed. The name was Emil Petersen.'

So Emil's surname was Petersen, I thought and asked, 'Why would he have been killed?'

'Beats me. I'm just repeating what I've heard. I was a boy during the Doctor Revolt, so all I know is what I've been told. Besides, I grew up in Hvannasund, so I can't claim to have experienced any of it at first hand.'

'Why are you in a wheelchair?' Haraldur asked.

'Sclerosis,' the man replied. 'Nothing wrong with my head, but the legs won't hold me and my arms don't have the strength they used to either. Who would've thought, I was chief engineer on one of the big prawn ships, and now I'm stuck here, a shadow of my former self, among mindless decrepit geriatrics.'

The latter was delivered as a statement of fact, without a trace of bitterness. Clearly a man who knew how to take the blows life deals you. And at this point I also noticed all the books scattered around the room, as well as paintings by young Faroese artists on the walls. I found one in particular, of a man in a suit with a guillemot head, both amusing and intriguing.

'You're looking at the paintings,' said the man in the wheelchair. 'They've become a passion of mine, and if I were in better shape I'd enrol to study art history. But I need round-the-clock care, so I can't do much other than this. Of course a wife could lend me a hand, then I might have a place somewhere, but where do you find a wife like that? As soon as the sclerosis started manifesting, mine wanted a divorce.'

He had a melancholy air now, but it was short-lived. 'Still, shouldn't complain, I've got enough money in the bank from the prawn days, so I can afford a taxi to cart me here and there to see the exhibitions.'

I got the impression that this man was probably better placed than many to identify who we should be talking to about those little fingers. But it meant having to tell him part of the story, so I did. When I was done, he pondered for a while.

'That doesn't sound like anything that could've happened in this country, but seeing as you're telling me this, I have to believe you. And now we know what came of my neighbour's Emil. Still, no reason to tell her. She's lived most of her life with that mystery. There's no reason to wrest the last sliver of hope away from her.' He examined us with a serious gaze.

'I also fully agree with you that there has to be some connection between those three skeletons.' He smiled apologetically: 'Those people, I mean. We know who they are after all. For my part, the issue is that I'm too young to have been involved back in the day, and now I'm too ill to be of any use. At least physically,' he added. 'Would've been good fun to get stuck in with you, but there's nothing for it.'

'You've never heard of people missing the tip of their little finger?' It was Haraldur who asked.

'No, I haven't. When I was out sailing many a man was a piece short of a finger here and there thanks to a slipped knife, but it can't be easy to hack off the tip of your left little finger by accident. When you find three people, or their remains, and they're all the tip of a left little finger short, it would appear to me that it was done on purpose.'

Both Karl and I had half formulated the same train of thought south in Tórshavn, but not as eloquently as this man at Norðoya Røktarheim.

33

At a restaurant near the care home Haraldur and I had wiener schnitzels and a beer, while we discussed what Dánjal Højgaard had told us. That was the name of the knowledgeable man in the wheelchair.

We'd spent more than an hour with him and he'd called for coffee and cake. When the young care assistant protested, saying it was only for residents, Dánjal replied she could put it on his tab. She could add a tip too, as long as she brought what he requested. Moments later a little trolley appeared in the middle of the room with a thermos of coffee, three types of tray bake, cups and plates.

'Please, help yourselves,' said the man in the wheelchair cheerfully. 'It's not every day I have guests over, and you should probably also have been offered a tipple, but I haven't any. The doctors tell me that because of my condition, I really shouldn't touch the stuff. However, I've started doubting how much of a difference it makes, so perhaps I should get a little buzz on every now and then.'

'Certainly worth a try,' chimed in Haraldur, who rarely refused a glass. 'My father used to say that spirits were the best of all the things that did nowt to ward off disease.'

We all laughed and the talk turned to Klaksvík in the 1950s. The one who knew the most was Dánjal Høgjaard. He was from up here, and so had heard many an account of those years, and he'd also read widely on the topic. Haraldur had been half-grown, and as a staunch supporter of independence he also had his piece to add. As for me, I didn't know much about that chapter in Faroese history, but I'd often heard people in Tórshavn say that the whole of Klaksvík had gone raving mad in those years. Which wasn't of much use. I'd also seen one of the TV programmes about the Klaksvík Revolt, but, to my shame, I'd been so hung-over that I'd dozed through most of it.

Dánjal Høgjaard told us that, as far as he'd understood it, the events were comparable to a civil war. That may, of course, be stretching the concept a little, but it had been citizen against citizen, town against town and country against country. At the same time the term *Klaksvík Revolt* was misleading, because in reality it had been a *Doctor Revolt*, which the authorities in Tórshavn had made a complete hash of.

The saga in a nutshell was that the Danish doctor Olaf Halvorsen had been a member of the Nazi party for two years, but had resigned when the Germans occupied Denmark. During the war he wanted to join the Eastern Front as a Red Cross medic, but that didn't work out. After the war the Danish Medical Association accused him of attempting to become an SS doctor. Halvorsen denied this and he was found not guilty, but sentenced to pay the legal costs of 601.50 kroner. Halvorsen refused to pay, he didn't think he'd done anything wrong. The Medical Association dug in its heels and so did Halvorsen, which meant that he lost the right to practise medicine in Denmark. He therefore ends up as a locum doctor in Klaksvík, but without paying the fine he isn't eligible for a permanent position. Halvorsen does his job well and in Klaksvík they are very fond of him and completely indifferent to his one-time membership of the Danish Nazi Party. Some people even maintained that if the Nazis were like Halvorsen, then they were nice blokes.

The authorities in Tórshavn then appoint a new doctor, but the locals in Klaksvík don't want him. They want Halvorsen, and that's none of the Danish Medical Association's business. In the winter of 1952-53 a petition was circulated in the village and it garnered a lot of support. Ninety-five per cent of adults signed it, and the remainder became known as Fivers. But you've heard of them?

Dánjal Høgjaard looked at us quizzically, and we both nodded. That much we knew. The man in the wheelchair continued:

'This generated bad blood in the village, and if you were a Fiver you were a Judas stabbing your own in the back. Like someone said, it was worse than ending up in hell. Their children didn't have an easy time at school either, because the other kids both taunted and threw stones at them. The newly appointed doctor's belongings were also shipped north, but the storage facility was broken into and the furniture smashed. As with so much else in those years, no culprit was ever found.

'Another Faroese doctor was already a GP up north, but because he didn't side with the majority, they gave him hell. A nanny had been down to the harbour with his little daughter in a pram and been told that it wouldn't be a sin to drown this little Fiver spawn. So that doctor upped sticks and left and then Halvorsen was stuck on his own looking after both the hospital and all of Norðoyggjar. The authorities tried to send two Danish doctors north as locum cover, but were informed that these two men must be tired of life, seeing as they intended to come to Klaksvík. On several occasions representatives of the authorities tried to come ashore in Klaksvík, but angry men stopped them landing.'

Dánjal Høgjaard smiled to himself. 'Klaksvík was like a republic, independent of the rest of the country. Even taxes were retained and not transferred south to Tórshavn, but spent instead here in the north. However, in 1955 the authorities lost patience with the lawlessness in Norðoyggjar and planned to arrest Halvorsen. The highest ranking officials in the country travelled north alongside representatives of the Faroese Government, but a crowd, which also knocked a few of them over, pushed them back on board the ferry *Tjaldur* and cut the hawsers. That was the final straw, and in spring 1955 the Danish authorities sent the ship *Parkeston* with 120 police officers on board to the Faroe Islands.

'Still the people of Klaksvík refused to submit and came to the conclusion that all that was left to do was give as good as they got. They moored two ships at the approach to the port and fashioned a floating barrier of barrels across the bay. Both ships and barrels were stuffed with gunpowder and dynamite.

They had a remote control, and if the *Parkeston* with its police officers approached, they swore they would blow up the entire contraption. The village was also crawling with armed men, many of the rifles were British, from the war, and people were pouring in from across the country to support Klaksvík.

'Be that as it may,' Dánjal Høgjaard continued, 'the Danish mediators managed to calm the waters sufficiently for the explosives to be removed. After criss-crossing the archipelago for a month, the *Parkeston* sailed back to Denmark, and Halvorsen left the country. In Klaksvík people believed he would return. He didn't. He was sick and tired of the turmoil and after this worked as a doctor first in Sweden, and then for the remainder of his life in Copenhagen.

'Later in the autumn representatives of the authorities made another journey north with the Danish High Commissioner at the helm, only this time locals had them locked in a house. That was one step too far for the Danish authorities. Their representative in the Faroes, along with other high-ranking gentlemen, was being held hostage in Klaksvík. Although the hostages were released fairly swiftly, the authorities refused to put up with this, and they now dispatched the frigate *Rolf Krake* to Klaksvík. The *Rolf Krake* was one of the largest ships in the Danish Navy and was carrying 32 police officers and 150 marines. Along with several dogs.

'In spite of skirmishes and resistance, the *Rolf Krake* forces its way to the quayside and the canine squad is sent ashore. Four weeks of disturbances follow in Klaksvík with bombs going off, policemen restraining protesters on the ground by force and dogs biting demonstrators. In the end a number of ringleaders are arrested and sent to Tórshavn where they are sentenced. Over the winter of 1955-56 the unrest gradually peters out.'

'So it was especially in 1955 that there were serious troubles in Klaksvík?' I asked.

'That's right. In the spring the bay is rigged with explosives and in the autumn several houses are blown up, and explosive devices are found underneath houses, bombs which for some reason don't go off. But it isn't just confined to Klaksvík.

The Prime Minister lives in Tvøroyri and shots are fired into his house, although nobody is injured. That's also one of the conclusions, in spite of all the weapons and violent rhetoric barely anyone is injured. Not seriously at least.'

'Halvorsen didn't return?' I asked finally.

'No, he didn't return, and it's probably in autumn 1955 when this becomes clear to everyone in Klaksvík, so they escalate too far. They think they've lost, and they did in a way, but the authorities in Tórshavn lost too. They shouldn't have listened to the Medical Association but applied their own common sense. Halvorsen was a good doctor and very popular, and as regards that fine, they could simply have ignored it.'

'That's what I've always said,' Haraldur exclaimed later at the restaurant. 'We voted for independence in 1946, and had it not been refused, none of this would've happened. Then it wouldn't be some lousy Danish Medical Association that decided who got a job in the Faroes and who didn't.'

'I'm really not going to get into all that about independence in 1946,' I said. 'We'll never see eye to eye anyway, but there's no doubt that the Danish Medical Association held too much sway.'

It was mid afternoon by now and we were gazing across the bay towards Stangabrúgv, which was gleaming in the sunshine.

'Time to pay a visit to that man Dánjal Høgjaard said knew everything worth knowing about the Doctor Revolt, as seen from Klaksvík.'

34

The man who opened the door was squat with dark grey hair and lively smiling eyes. I estimated his age as somewhere in his late seventies, but he seemed sprightly.

'Good afternoon,' Haraldur said. We'd agreed that it would be best if he did the introductions. 'Dánjal Højgaard told us you were the person to talk to if we wanted to know anything about the Doctor Revolt.'

Dánjal Høgjaard had urged us not to say Klaksvík Revolt, but Doctor Revolt, because that was the term used by most people in Klaksvík.

'He's right on that count. If there's anything you want to know about that scandal, then I likely know more than most,' he said with a smile. 'Do come into the living room, so we can have a cup of coffee.'

Haraldur and I winked at each other; we hadn't ordered coffee at the restaurant, as we were certain that, if we made it through the door, we'd be guaranteed coffee and cake.

The stocky man, who we were informed was named Hans Petur Mørkøre, walked briskly ahead of us while chatting away. 'How was Dánjal?' And before we had a chance to reply, he followed up with: 'It's a bloody shame such a gifted man as Dánjal should get that terrible disease. We were on a couple of expeditions together in Greenland. I've hardly met a more knowledgeable man in my life.'

We entered a living room where every wall was clad in timber and unadorned, bar two paintings of Klaksvík. The man of the house clearly considered the wood itself to be so warm and vibrant that no more was needed.

'Now they're telling me that this illness, sclerosis, only exists here among us who are descended from the Vikings. That immune defence which made Norsemen so hardy has turned against us. I swear it's only because in our days we've grown weak at the knees.'

We nodded in agreement at his words, saying nothing.

He invited us to take an armchair each, and then he'd fetch coffee and biscuits. His wife had sadly passed three years ago, so he was alone in the house.

He was soon back and set the table. 'I always have coffee in the thermos. It's a habit from the watches on board where we used to drink coffee so strong we had to take care not to spill any on the ship's deck, in case it burned clean through.' His laughter revealed a set of gleaming white dentures.

After we'd sampled the coffee and each picked a biscuit, he asked, 'So, what is it you want to know?'

'Dánjal Høgjaard told us about the Kla… the Doctor Revolt,' I managed to correct myself in the nick of time, and I could feel Haraldur glaring at me. 'Neither Haraldur nor I are particularly well informed, but we know that the authorities both in Denmark and the Faroes committed a grave injustice against the people of Klaksvík.' I thought it best to humour the man first if we wanted to find anything out.

'They most certainly did,' he said in a loud and animated voice. 'It's without any doubt the greatest injustice ever committed on these shores. But have we ever had any apology?' He looked me straight in the eye. 'No we have not.' The latter was said with emphasis. Then he carried on in a more subdued tone: 'Not that it matters much any more, barely anyone from that time is alive today. My own blood also ran hotter back then. It's like you grow milder over the years.'

'You've heard of Ísak Joensen, who was found dead on the shore of Fagralíð?' I asked.

'Indeed I have, and I've also heard that he was allegedly chained, so he drowned when the tide rose.'

'It's true,' I said. 'He suffered a terrifying death.'

'Horrific. Tragic to think that the pair of us stood shoulder to shoulder in the battles against the police and the navy back in the day.' He fell quiet for a moment, then added: 'A terrible way to go.'

'Did you also know Emil Petersen?'

'Yes of course I knew Emil, but he disappeared. I heard rumours that he was hiding in Suðuroy. But that was many decades ago.'

'We found his skeleton down south.' I didn't think there was any reason to say that we'd only found one arm.

'How did he die?'

'We don't know, but it was probably just as unpleasant as for Ísak.'

The smile that had been plastered on Hans Petur Mørkøre's face was gone.

'Did you also know Maud Simonsen?'

'Yeah,' he said in a faint voice. 'Is she dead too?'

'She is, and in roughly the same way as Ísak and Emil.'

He cradled his face in his hands and shook his head, saying: 'I didn't want to believe it, though somewhere deep down I've known all along that it was so. That they were dead. That maybe it was so.'

He looked up from his hands. 'You're absolutely certain that it's these people you've found? I know that Ísak wasn't difficult to identify, but the others?'

'Do you know anything about why all three of them were missing the tip of their left little finger?' I asked, and I could tell from his expression that I'd hit the nail on the head.

'Then it's them,' he said, so softly I could barely hear him.

'Who were they? Why were they missing that joint?'

Hans Petur Mørkøre leaned back in the sofa and stared at the ceiling as he replied: 'They were all *Niners*.'

'*Niners*? What's that? I've heard of *Fivers* and *Ninety-fivers*, but not of *Niners*.'

'That's because it was a secret society fighting for Klaksvík to become an autonomous part of the Faroe Islands.'

35

'When the battle heated up in earnest in 1955, there were some of us who decided there was no backing down now,' Hans Petur Mørkøre recounted. 'We held secret meetings where we also invited a couple of women along. Among them Maud Simonsen, who'd proven her courage and resolve. At first the fight was about Halvorsen staying at Klaksvík Hospital. That's why we deployed mines, and that's why we packed *Barm* and *Svínoyar-Bjarni* with dynamite and the watchmaker made us a wireless detonator, so we were ready in case the Danes got too close with a battleship. We also blew up a couple of houses belonging to those traitor devils, the *Fivers*, and we attempted to blow up the house of a member of parliament, but that unfortunately failed.

'Later, when it became clear that Halvorsen had left for good, we were incensed, and we took a couple of public officials hostage. Still, we didn't harm them and let them go after a day or so. I can tell you this, when they were locked up there wasn't much bravado about them. I don't know if they thought we might shoot them.' Hans Petur smiled. 'You have to remember, this wasn't that long after the end of the war and so many people did get killed in various ways back then. People were used to thinking along those lines, and in Denmark they'd only just completed the task of executing traitors. Perhaps it wasn't so far-fetched that they feared for their lives.'

'More coffee, anyone?' asked the friendly Klaksvík man, who'd been involved in holding both the Danish High Commissioner and Chief of Police as hostages.

When we didn't accept the offer he added, 'I haven't anything else to offer you. I took an oath to abstain in my early youth, and I'm not about to betray it.'

Haraldur and I glanced at each other and shared a thought.

'People usually say that it was the last straw for the authorities when we took those hostages, but I can tell you that it was the last straw for us when we heard that the *Rolf Krake* was on its way crammed to the gunwales with policemen and dogs. At that point six of us held a top-secret meeting where we agreed that we would never back down. From this meeting on we called ourselves *Niners*, but never mentioned it to anyone. We were four men and two women, and I can tell you this: they were the most ruthless.'

'Why *Niners*? There were only six of you,' asked Haraldur.

'At first we planned on calling ourselves *Sixers*, but then someone thought that made it sound as if we were playing Ludo. At this point Christian Jensen suggested that we should call ourselves *Niners*.'

'Who's Christian Jensen?' I asked.

'He was a young man from the town, who was studying theology in Denmark and was home for the summer holidays. He disappeared along with the others.'

I was about to fire off more questions, when Haraldur indicated that it was best to ask as little as possible and let the man talk.

'Christian told us that nine was a number with magical properties, which in Hebrew meant truth. I also clearly recall him saying it was a number that renewed itself: two times 9 is 18, and 1 plus 8 is 9, just as 3 times 9 is 27, and 2 plus 7 is 9, and so on. According to Christian, this meant that the truth will always be revealed in the end. We were Christians, like just about everyone in Klaksvík, and we liked the Biblical touch'.

'What was with the little finger?' I couldn't help myself, I had to ask.

'That came a little later in autumn, when I wasn't part of it any more. Shortly after we founded the society, I was offered hire on a trawler from Tórshavn setting out to fish the waters northwest of Iceland in mid-winter. So there I was. It was hard to find a hire, and I had a new house full of children. My wife said there was nothing to discuss. If I didn't take the hire we'd lose the house, and then she'd leave and take the children with her. It was a bitter pill to swallow, but although I felt like a traitor, I went to Tórshavn and boarded the trawler. I only said goodbye to my wife and little ones. No one else.'

For a moment the old man was lost in his own thoughts, then he said: 'I can promise you I was on the verge of tears many a time when I went to sleep in my berth. As long as we were busy, I couldn't think too much, but when I didn't pass out as soon as my head hit the pillow, my thoughts wouldn't fly to my wife and kids, but to my brothers in arms. I swear if I could choose again, I would've chosen to stay in Klaksvík.' He looked determined. 'That's how bad I felt about my decision. When news reached us that it was all over, and that the Danish ship had returned to Denmark with its men and dogs, I didn't know what to make of it. I certainly wasn't happy.'

After a brief pause he resumed: 'We returned to port some-time in mid March, and only Christian Jensen was left of my brothers in arms. But he wasn't the Christian I'd left. He was scared witless, he'd barely speak a word to me, didn't dare to. He was pale as a corpse and so thin that he rattled inside his hide. I asked after the others, but he said they'd fled Klaksvík and gone into hiding. I asked why, and he said that someone wanted to kill them all. He didn't know who was behind it, but he knew it was serious, because Marianna had already been killed.'

'Who is Marianna?' I asked.

'Marianna was the other woman in the society, but Chris-tian refused to say a word about how she died. It wasn't until I swore that I'd bash his face in myself if he didn't tell me that his tongue loosened. They'd found Marianna dead in a little cave in the bay of Borðoyarvík, right below where her parents had a field. She was chained naked inside the cave and into her back was carved *Just wait!* The three who were left had no doubt that their end was near. So they decided to flee Klaksvík and hide until it was over.'

'Why would someone want to kill them?' This was Haraldur.

'I couldn't get it out of him. He refused to spit it out, but he was clearly ashamed of something. I also noticed that he was missing the tip of his little finger, and I asked him how that happened. He told me that after I ran away – those were the words he used – the others who stayed behind became even closer. They undertook more daring attacks, such as trying to assassinate the Faroese Prime Minister. That plan failed, but someone else was blamed and thrown in prison. At a meeting where they'd been drinking steadily, they decided that their secret mark should be that they'd sacrificed the tip of their left little finger. So one after the other they had the tip chopped off with an axe. He also said that they'd later realised it was foolish, but by then it was too late.'

'Bloody hell,' Haraldur said. 'If we'd had more such fire-brands in 1946, there's no way the Danes would've been allowed to steal the referendum from us.'

'You too want the Faroes free?' asked the old northern islander.

'Do I ever,' Haraldur replied. 'I've no desire to live off Danish charity.'

'Shake my hand, brother,' Hans Petur Mørkøre said. 'We wholeheartedly agree there.'

This wasn't exactly my cup of tea, so I asked if Marianna's death had been reported?

'No, it wasn't reported. Her parents were ashamed of what happened to their daughter, and we northerners weren't exactly on great terms with the police. Christian told me that she'd been buried quietly, without any fuss made of how she died.'

'How did she die?' I asked.

'She froze to death. Naked, her back a gaping wound and in mid winter,' the Klaksvík man said quietly.

'What became of this Christian?' Haraldur jumped in.

'Shortly after we spoke he disappeared. I tried asking around, but never really got an answer.'

'So you've no idea what became of him?' Haraldur asked, looking straight into the old man's eyes.

'No, I don't know what became of him, but I did hear a story that I find hard to believe.'

'And what story was this?' Haraldur continued his questioning.

'A man who'd been out fishing with an inshore boat that usually landed its catch in Eiði village, swore that one afternoon shortly before dusk he had seen Christian on board a boat right by Stallurin on the north side of Eysturoy.'

'How did he manage to recognise Christian? I don't suppose the fishing boat was sailing close to land.'

'No, they were cruising towards Klaksvík, but he'd been passing the time with a pair of binoculars. At some point he spotted a little boat near land by the Stallurin landing place, and a man was asleep in the stern. He was pretty certain that the guy was Christian Jensen.'

'Then what happened?' I asked.

'He lowered the binoculars to tell the others on board, and when he raised them to look again, the little boat was gone.'

'He could just have been imagining things in the dwindling twilight,' Haraldur said.

'That's what I said, but he insisted. He'd tried to get the other two to sail the boat close to land, but they refused. They wanted to go home and didn't feel like chasing ghosts.'

'And you didn't do anything about it?' I said.

'No, why would I. At first maybe I sided with the bloke who said he'd seen Christian, but when I thought about it, I realised that it sounded pretty far-fetched.'

'Isn't there a grotto near Stallurin?' asked Haraldur.

'Yeah,' Hans Petur Mørkøre replied. 'A seal cave, Látursgjógv they call it.'

Kelp Forests Languidly Waft

Now eve falls on cliff ledge and toft,
clover its dainty leaves laces.
And kelp forests languidly waft,
as night these islands embraces.

36

We cruised past Búgvin and Haraldur told me about the feats performed there. How hard it was to get up on that sea stack, and that it wasn't just anyone who could accomplish it. That a few years back there'd been a rockslide down the cliff face, and that Búgvin was now connected to the island.

'But it won't last long, I promise you that. When it's blowing northerly the breakers crash so hard against the cliff that a rockslide like that gets cleared away. Mark my words, in a few years' time we'll be sailing all the way around Búgvin again.'

Haraldur knew his bearings up north and he entertained us with anecdotes all the way out to Stallurin.

The original plan had been to drive back to Tórshavn, but as we were motoring beneath the crags by Valaknúkar in Skálabotnur, Haraldur had said out of the blue: 'Do you know the story of the Floksmen?'

'Sure, they were bandits in the olden days who thought they could pillage and murder as they pleased.'

'Precisely, and they took a blood oath on their alliance, just like The Niners chopped the tip off their little fingers.'

'As far as I recall, they were sentenced to death and pushed off Valaknúkar,' I added.

'They got their due,' Haraldur said. 'That's the point here. Whoever killed The Niners might get away scot-free.'

'I think you're getting everything jumbled up now. The Floksmen were brutal bastards and were condemned, while The Niners might have been hard-headed vandals, but they were never sentenced, just killed.'

'Precisely,' Haraldur said, and I gave up on trying to understand his figurative language.

'There's someone out there,' he pressed on, 'probably more than the one person, who's executed people without judge or jury. If we don't do something about it, it'll be like in Roncevaux.'

'In *Roncevaux*?' I asked. I couldn't fathom the connection.

'Yes, what's right and what's wrong is decided by force of arms.'

'But didn't the Twelve Paladins win the Battle of Roncevaux Pass?'

'Precisely,' Haraldur repeated, this time with emphasis. 'That's why I think we should drive up to Gjógv and get someone to sail us out from the village to the Látursgjógv cave.'

I may not have grasped Haraldur's analogies, but I understood he was being serious and so, instead of driving on up to the tunnel, I turned off towards Funningsfjørður and Gjógv.

After a silence I asked Haraldur: 'How come you've turned into such a crusader for justice?'

He seemed to ponder this for a minute, and then replied: 'Sanna and I have been a couple for years, but now that we've spent months in the Mediterranean we've been together talking from early morning till late at night. She told me what goes on out at Tinganes. How politicians and officials couldn't care less about how much public money they spend. There's no ceiling on expensive flights and equally expensive hotel suites. The public coffers pay, and that means you and I. Droves of directors don't do a day's work, they just jet around the world for their pleasure. Your average Joe foots the bill.'

Now he'd really worked himself up. 'It can't go on! It has to stop!'

'Hence we have to do our utmost to solve these murders?'

'Precisely!' Haraldur replied with determination.

This might have been my strangest ever conversation with Haraldur, and I wasn't sure there was much coherence to any of what was said. On the other hand, it was abundantly clear that he believed it necessary to dig out the rot both here and there. And that suited me just fine, I was a journalist after all and happy to oblige.

So here we were approaching Stallurin in a wooden four-man Faroe boat. Haraldur's relative, who we'd roped into this detour, said that the sea was so calm that it should be possible to enter the gorge.

The relative from Gjógv turned the engine down to near idling, and slowly we approached. Gradually the cliff face ahead rose, until it towered like a titanic wall greeting us with gaping mouth. Once we slipped inside it went dark very quickly, but we had our torches with us and lit up ahead. The sea swell boomed, like in a gigantic hall, and blended with the cautious clicks of the engine. Slowly, slowly we sailed further and further in, but there was still no end to the gorge.

'I went all the way in once, there's a sandbank,' the local said. 'It was shortly after the war, we were a handful of youths who explored all the caves along this side one fine summer's day. I remember the jitters we got when the light from the entrance faded, and we only had a paltry torch with us.'

For a while we sailed wordlessly in the temple-like harmonies of the sea. The gorge soon closed in until we could touch the walls on both sides.

'As far as I recall, it isn't much further,' said our guide.

As he'd said the words, the sand bank appeared in our torch beams. It wasn't wide, like an average living room floor, and it looked empty.

We sailed so close that the keel touched the seabed, and then we let the engine idle. We didn't have the nerve to turn it off.

It definitely wasn't quiet in here, but the sounds that now dominated, apart from the nearly soundless motor, bore testament to the unbridled forces of nature.

'This is like being in St. Peter's Basilica in Rome,' Haraldur whispered.

'Yes, only bigger,' I replied, and Haraldur nodded.

We both climbed to the bow and lowered ourselves onto the sand, while the man from Gjógv stayed on board. He thought it wisest as the tide would soon be turning and the waters would grow choppy. At that point we'd have to hurry out of here if we held our lives dear.

The white sand gleamed, but there was no skeleton in sight. Not of human or animal. Right up against the cave wall lay a deposit of cobblestones, and we swept it with our beams to check if there was anything to find there. But no, sand and cobbles, that was all.

'I guess we've checked this out now,' Haraldur said, and I could hear the disappointment in his voice. 'At least this particular stone hasn't been left unturned.'

He quickly followed up with: 'Though it would've been more fun if we'd found some trace of Christian Jensen. But it wasn't to be.'

'I wouldn't quite say that,' I replied, pointing my torch at the rock wall above the cobbles. 'What d'you reckon that is?'

The shaft of light lit up a short chain which was bolted to the wall, and from its end dangled a shackle.

37

It was ten in the evening when I dropped Haraldur off á Reyni and thanked him for his help. He, in turn, said that he'd had a great day and any time.

At the station I was told that Karl had just gone home, but he'd left instructions to contact him on the mobile if anything urgent cropped up. I returned to the car and phoned him.

Karl sounded sleepy when he picked up: 'Karl Olsen.'

'It's Hannis. Sorry for waking you, but at the station they told me I could call.'

'That's all right, Hannis. I'd just nodded off in front of the telly. There've been too many late nights. So, did you two find anything out in Klaksvík?'

I was surprised he knew it wasn't just me who'd gone north, and I replied, 'How d'you know I wasn't alone in Klaksvík?'

'You may well think that we're oafs in the force, but we're not so sodding hopeless that we don't know when two blokes from Tórshavn are doing the rounds of care homes scaring pensioners witless.'

'We didn't...'

'You idiot, you're so easy to wind up it almost isn't worth it. Bergur Mjóvanes visited his relative Dánjal Højgaard yesterday at Norðoya Røktarheim, and he told him of a visit he'd received. He also said that this fine pair were nearly the death of the lady next door to him, and that they'd been chattering about little fingers.'

'Then Bergur also told you that we were sent to see Hans Petur Mørkøre.'

'He did and he went the same way, but the bugger wouldn't open the door for him, though Bergur swears he was in. They've butted heads more than once, so Bergur figured that was probably why. But you and Haraldur, did you two manage a word with Hans Petur the secessionist?'

'Why'd you call him that?'

'That's what they call him up north, seeing as he's forever going around claiming that the Danish authorities have no place in the Faroes since we seceded in 1946.'

'I see,' I laughed. 'He and Haraldur did agree on that count.'

'Can imagine,' Karl scoffed. 'But you've a story to tell then, and time is short. It's only half ten, so come on over and tell me what you and the two secessionists figured out.'

'Over to yours?' I said, and a shiver ran up my spine.

'Why not? I'll make sure Katrin doesn't kill you. I have a fowling shotgun on top of a closet somewhere; I can defend you with that. Where the pellets are I've no idea, but there's no need for Katrin to know that.'

'Easy for you to say, and it's a low blow too. I'm the one who's in for a hiding.'

'Don't be such a dishrag! Man up and come over, right now. I might even have something for us to wet our lips.'

He hung up.

38

With quaking heart I drove the short stretch up to Stoffalág where Karl and Katrin's house was. I rang the doorbell and mercifully it was Karl who opened the door and let me into the living room.

'I appear to be low on single malt at the moment, but I did find a heeltap of eighteen-year-old Glenlivet.' He handed me a tumbler with about an inch of whisky, and I said *skál* and had a taste.

'Not too shabby,' I said, scanning the surroundings to see if Katrin was in sight. She wasn't.

'If it's Katrin you're looking for, she just drove off.'

'Because I arrived?'

'Yeah, because you're here.' Karl paused for a moment. 'She's gone to the shop down on Jónas Broncksgøta to buy something to go with the coffee she's intending to offer you.'

I could breathe a little easier knowing that I had a momentary reprieve, but I fully expected to be getting an earful before long.

'Tell me what that clown Hans Petur Mørkøre told you. He ought to know about the little fingers.'

'He did,' I said, and recapped everything he told us. To conclude I narrated the trip into Látursgjógv, where we'd found a chain with an iron shackle, but no bones.

'The surf probably cleared them out,' Karl remarked.

'The guy from Gjógv who sailed us in, claimed that up north the breakers can be ferocious, nothing that isn't bolted down stays put. Christian Jensen was no doubt shackled to the cliff like the others and died in there. He disappeared in early 1956, and that makes it 55 years ago. It's nothing short of a miracle that the chain was still there in the gorge.'

'It's a grim affair,' Karl said, 'and that secessionist devil in Klaksvík won't get away with not telling us what he knows. It would appear that while he was fishing somewhere between Iceland and Greenland, the remaining Niners took things a step too far.'

Karl had a gulp of whisky and carried on, 'And what kind of foolish drivel is it to create a secret society and call it The Niners, because the number nine is *magical.*' Those last words came out with a splutter. 'And as icing on the cake they hack off the tip of their left little fingers to show that they belong to this society.'

'My guess is that they lived it all more intensely, more seriously than we understand it today,' I said. 'Don't forget that this wasn't long after the war, and in Klaksvík they'd been living in a pseudo state of war for years. Under those circumstances it's easy to wall yourself off in a peculiar secret world with a certain set of enemies and special rules. Then it can seem natural to create a society with its own rituals. Like chopping the tip off a little finger.'

'The hell would I know,' Karl replied. 'They definitely weren't right in the head. And what on earth did they do which was so horrific that they've all been murdered, one after the other. Four of them right after the Klaksvík Revolt and the final one last week. It's hard to make sense of this,' he said, shaking his head.

'What's the matter now, love?' It was Katrin, who was standing in the kitchen doorway. 'Hello, Hannis!'

'Hi Katrin,' I mustered in as carefree a tone as possible, but the words nearly stuck in my throat.

'It's these murder cases,' Karl said, fortunately for me, because I didn't know what else to say. 'We're having a hard time making head or tail of it all,' he added.

'I'm sure you'll figure it out,' Katrin said. Her thoughts were clearly elsewhere. 'Coffee, Hannis?'

'Yes, please,' I replied politely, and Katrin went back to the kitchen and closed the door behind her.

'Well, well, old friend,' Karl joked. 'You survived the first round.'

'I'd expected her to tear into me, but behaving as if nothing has happened is almost worse.' I shuddered. 'It's verging on the sinister.'

Karl just chuckled.

Moments later he picked up where he had left off. 'Then there's Áki Hansen who tried to murder you, but wound up dead himself shortly after, and then someone else snatched the arm from you south in Trongisvágur.'

'I never had the arm,' I protested, 'but it's true that I touched the canvas bag before I was knocked out. The footprint in the dust on the floor in Trongisvágur and the one at home in my kitchen were the same.'

'We've examined both, and you're right. The prints were left by the same shoe. But we're probably not looking for a tall man, it was just a size 42.'

'Most men in this country wear size 42 footwear, so that doesn't tell us much.'

'No, maybe not,' Karl said, 'but at least it's something tangible. And it's just about all we have to go on.'

Then Katrin reappeared with coffee and a couple of slices of brioche with cheese.

'I thought the pastries they had left looked a little boring, so I bought a French bread instead. Right, here's a midnight snack if you fancy one.' She placed the tray on the sofa table and as she passed me, she stroked my cheek.

I was so taken aback that my face flushed bright red and Karl started chortling. Katrin disappeared back into the kitchen.

'You look like you've seen a ghost in broad daylight.'

Eventually I managed to stammer: 'I don't get it. What's she playing at?'

'Katrin isn't playing at anything, she's always liked you, and she simply wants to show you that.'

'Yeah, but it was my impression that not long ago she swore to maim me if I showed my face here.'

'That may be true, but you shouldn't always take what women say so literally. They often mean something else.'

'But this is a seachange,' I said shakily.

'Not inconceivable,' Karl replied, as if it were of minor consequence.

For a moment he was lost in his own thoughts; then he said: 'Looking back at recent events, we'll have to go back to the Klaksvík Revolt to find the motive.'

'D'you think the murders have something to do with the Klaksvík Revolt?'

'Yes and no. The murders aren't part of that conflict, but rather a consequence of events that took place during the unrest.'

'Which events?'

'We don't know. But that's what we need to find out and I think we have the right man for it.'

39

It was nearly ten in the morning when I woke up. The state of the house was the same as before my trip north to Klaksvík, because I'd arrived home so late that I was too tired to do anything about anything. I showered and got dressed, had coffee, there wasn't much else in the house, and called a glazier to come and replace the pane in the front door. Most of what had been smashed on the kitchen floor I binned, and then I moved on to the living room and tried my best to return it to some semblance of order. The chairs I righted, returned books to shelves, and put LPs and CDs back where they belonged. Still, a lot was wrecked, not just the computer. The tonearm was torn off my old record player, and the CD player had been thrown on the floor too. I put it back on the shelf and plugged it in. It bloody worked! Hallur Joensen with his song 'Gyltar Ljósakrúnur' flooded the room.

Singing along, I'd picked the last things up off the floor.

'If it were me, I'd let Hallur sing solo.' Bergur Mjóvanes grinned at me from the doorway. 'Your voice isn't exactly a match for his.'

'I'm aware of that,' I said, turning down the volume a notch.

'Feel up for a road trip to Klaksvík?' Bergur asked, and looked searchingly at me with his grey eyes.

'I was in Klaksvík only yesterday, so I think I've had quite enough for now.'

'Karl doesn't think so, and I actually think I might agree with him there.'

'Why? What have the two of you cooked up?' I glanced at him with distrust.

'I gather from Karl that the two of you have been downing whisky and solving murder mysteries in the Faroe Isles. Or rather that you *didn't* solve any murder mysteries in the Faroe Isles, because you didn't know what triggered the chain of events.'

'And?' I shot back.

'Karl and I are convinced that Hans Petur Mørkøre didn't tell you and Haraldur the truth. At least not the whole of it. I know that bloody-minded git, he knows more than he's letting on.'

Karl hadn't wanted to tell me who he was referring to when he mentioned 'the right man', but he'd said I would find out in due course. Clearly that man was Bergur Mjóvanes.

'But what d'you need me for in Klaksvík? I don't really get it.'

'When you two spoke yesterday, he told you a very long story. Now you're coming with me and we'll get him to retell the same story and hopefully quite a bit more. Given that you've heard the account before, you'll notice if he strays today from what he said yesterday. You see, the trouble with lying is that it's hard to remember what you've said. If you stick to the truth, there's rarely any doubt, but when you make things up, you quickly make a hash of it.'

'I'd planned on tidying today. Look at the state of this place.'

Bergur Mjóvanes looked around, 'Oh, I don't know. It's not much different from my son's room. He's eighteen,' he added.

He turned halfway and said, 'Come on, let's go, it's not like this is going to go anywhere.'

I sighed and plodded after the detective.

40

We drove north in an unmarked police car. There was a CD player in the car, and Bergur rummaged through the glove compartment until he pulled out a CD.

'I knew it,' he said with a victorious grin and showed me a cover with an image of Hallur Joensen. 'The young colleagues who often drive this car are absolutely nuts about country music.' All the way from Tórshavn north to Klaksvík we played the Faroese country king.

When we got out of the car at Hans Petur Mørkøre's place, I noticed a twitch of the curtains in one of the windows, but when we rang the doorbell nobody answered.

Bergur Mjóvanes took a few steps back from the house and bellowed in a voice that rang clear across the entire neighbourhood: 'If you don't open up this instant, Hans Petur, you'll regret it. We'll kick in the door and we'll throw you in a cell!'

The word *cell* was still bouncing back and forth between the nearby house walls as the front door opened and Hans Petur Mørkøre stuck his head out. 'What kind of spectacle is this?' He was riled-up. 'D'you intend to break into a decent man's home?'

'Don't you give me any bollocks about decency,' Bergur barked. 'If there's anything you're *not*, it's a decent man. Beggars belief that you can utter that word with a straight face. But you're probably so brazen you're not even familiar with the concept of shame.'

'Don't you get started with me, you thug from Eysturoy Island,' began Hans Petur, but Bergur just pushed past him and went inside. I followed on his heels.

Each in an armchair in the living room, we'd made ourselves quite comfortable by the time Hans Petur stormed in with a furious expression: 'Who on God's green earth gave you a licence to force yourselves into the home of an elderly widower.' He was trying to sound angry and to grovel at the same time, without much luck.

'Oh, shut it,' was the reply he got from Bergur Mjóvanes. 'If you don't cooperate, I can promise that you will do time. I know enough about you and your ways to get you locked away for years. What about that ewe you stole over in Múli?'

'I'm no sheep thief. You don't have any witnesses.' He looked livid standing there in the living room.

'Put a sock in it!' Bergur retorted. 'I've got at least three men willing to swear that they saw you manoeuvring that ewe into your car. Maybe I should just tell that lot over in Múli where their livestock disappeared to. You wouldn't live out the year.'

It was obvious that Hans Petur Mørkøre's first impulse was fury, but at the same time he grasped that he'd been checkmated, so he changed tack. 'I'm just an elderly man in poor health. There's no reason to be so rough,' he said with feigned frailty.

'Please, spare us the theatrics and take a seat over there.' Bergur pointed at the sofa.

Hans Petur Mørkøre sat himself down on the sofa and looked at the policeman. He hadn't deigned to glance at me once.

'This man, Hannis Martinsson, came here with another man yesterday to talk to you, and you told him about the society The Niners. You were one of the founders, but had the good fortune to be away when a misdeed was committed. Now you're going to tell me what that deed was.'

'I said to the pair of them yesterday.' He looked at me now. 'I was never told what happened while I was away.'

'So you didn't talk to Christian Jensen when you returned?'

'No, yes.' He glanced my way again. 'I met him on the street and saw that the tip of his left little finger was missing. I asked him how that happened and he told me they'd chopped it off to demonstrate their strength. Christian, who was well read, said it was like those Mensur scars among the Germans in the eighteenth century.'

He didn't mention that yesterday, I thought to myself, but kept quiet.

'You know that all the other members of The Niners have been murdered? All except you.' Bergur Mjóvanes ploughed on.

'I'm aware of that. But I didn't have anything to do with any of what they did. I wasn't even here.'

'Did Christian tell you what they'd done?'

'No, I never asked him about it. I didn't know a thing, I just supposed the others ran away.'

'But you knew that Marianna was murdered.' Bergur stared straight into Hans Petur Mørkøre's eyes.

'No, yes, I found out later.'

'Who told you?'

'I don't recall.'

'Yesterday you said that Christian Jensen told you,' I interjected.

'Could well be, I don't remember.'

'You don't remember if it was Christian who told you about Marianna?' Bergur asked.

'No, I don't.' He stood up. 'What is this? I won't put up with the third degree in my own house.'

'Sit down!' The order from the detective was so clear and emphatic that the old man sat promptly. 'It appears to me that you have a hard time remembering what is what, and it's no doubt because you're sitting here lying to our faces. You know full well what the other five got up to while you were away. You might as well tell us, because we're not going anywhere until you do.'

The stocky man, who had appeared so buoyant yesterday, now looked utterly dejected. He sat hunched on the sofa staring at the floor. Then it came softly:

'They killed a little girl.'

41

The remaining members of the society The Niners had taken to heavy drinking. They were behind bomb attacks on several houses, and they attempted to blast a hole in the side of the *Rolf Krake*. The attempt on the vessel failed for various reasons, and the Danes then moored the ship they were using to hold prisoners at the side of the *Rolf Krake*. If anything were to happen to the Danish frigate, then the Faroese captives would be blown up first. All this, coupled with the fact that both the police and navy were out to get them, put them under immense pressure. That's why they hit the bottle, to dull their nerves. On a night like that, where they were more than half pissed, they'd worked themselves up against The Fivers. Why should they be let off so easily? They were traitors of the worst sort, had no right to call themselves *klaksvíkingar*, had no right to live. One had said that they should never ever have released the Danish High Commissioner and the Chief of Police, but kept them hostage until the Danes and their lackeys from Tórshavn fled. At that point someone else suggested that they should take a Fiver hostage.

The others immediately agreed, and then they started discussing who it should be. They quickly agreed that the big merchant Weihe, one of the most ardent Fivers, deserved to be captured, and so they decided that they would catch him the next evening.

In the afternoon the following day, after dark, they staked out his home. By the time they'd waited almost two hours and were chilled to the bone, and still hadn't seen any merchant, they started to grow impatient. And the bottle was, of course, near to hand. At that point Weihe's little daughter came skipping by. She was singing and playing with a ball. There were no streetlights, they'd made sure of that days ago when they blew up the electrical substation. Not a word was spoken, they'd brought a rag and chloroform, and they pressed it over the child's nose and mouth. One, two, three and she was out cold, and they carried her to a basement not far away. They kept her unconscious there all night while they debated what to do with her. Christian Jensen, who'd told Hans Petur the story, claimed that he'd said that she should be released, but the others were against it. They hadn't nabbed the merchant, but he should still feel the sting.

The plan was never to harm the girl; she was just a means to demonstrate that there were powerful forces in Klaksvík, forces that didn't shy away from brutal methods. They therefore decided that she should be shackled in a cave on the shore nearby, where the Kósavirkið fish-filleting plant is now. They'd leave her there for a couple of hours, and then they'd inform the parents.

Hans Petur Mørkøre looked up at us. We said nothing, so he carried on:

'Tragically for both the girl and the members of The Niners, that same evening another group made a second attempt to blast a hole in the side of the *Rolf Krake*. They'd filled a barrel with gunpowder and dynamite, and when the explosives were close to the prison ship, they cut the ship loose and let it drift out of the bay. The problem was that the barrel floated after the ship, and when it had drifted out a little the wake of another boat that was trying to catch the prison ship sent it even further. Eventually it was near the cave where the girl was shackled, and that was the moment the crew that had floated the barrel picked to press the wireless detonator. That way at least the Danes wouldn't get their hands on the barrel of dynamite. The girl could probably have survived the blast, but misfortune would have it that someone had thrown a fistful of four-inch nails in with the explosives. Several of them pierced the ten-year-old girl, and according to Christian Jensen, the wounds were fatal.'

There wasn't much vigour left in the old man from Klaksvík. He sat hunched and pale on the sofa, his face drained of all the life it radiated yesterday.

42

Shortly after the tragedy with his daughter, Weihe shut up shop and moved to Denmark, and that's all Hans Petur Mørkøre knew of him. He didn't know the identity of those who'd taken the lives of the members of The Niners, and he said that Christian Jensen hadn't known either. They just assumed that they'd been ruthless Fivers, or, and Hans Petur was convinced of this, Danish secret police.

'The way the Danes have treated us for centuries, it wouldn't surprise me in the least,' he'd declared.

Bergur had told him to shut up and asked if it was also the Danes who'd shackled Ísak Joensen to the shore? To that, Hans Petur didn't reply.

The Weihe family vanished so suddenly that nothing was done to investigate their daughter's ordeal, and in general hardly anything was cleared up. Klaksvík was in a state of emergency and the police held little sway.

On the road south, Bergur Mjóvanes and I attempted to make sense of what we knew, but there were several unanswered questions. A girl's tragic fate during the Klaksvík Revolt had triggered a series of events in which members of the secret society The Niners had been killed. However, we still didn't know who was behind the killings then. And when we arrived at the present day, there was even less clarity. It's true that Ísak Joensen had hidden in Iceland for over fifty years, but as soon as he set foot back in Klaksvík he'd been killed. There was surely a direct link back to the Klaksvík Revolt, but the same men could hardly have perpetrated the murders then and now. Another loose end was Áki Hansen, who'd tried to finish me off, but had been found shortly after with his throat slit. And who had knocked me out in Trongisvágur?

The questions still outnumbered the answers, and I hadn't even mentioned the incident at the hospital to Bergur, where someone had tried to make their way into Edmund's room late at night.

I'd intended to have a meeting with Karl, but Bergur Mjóvanes thought that from now on I could relax and stay out of it. They would definitely send for me if they needed me. Who knew? Maybe they would decide to publish an in-house magazine for staff. And should that be the case, it wasn't unlikely the force would get in touch with me, he said with a grin and dropped me off on Jóanes Paturssonargøta.

It riled me, but I also knew that those were the conditions. I wasn't actually on the police payroll, so any insight I gained was at their discretion.

I strolled up to the mini market in the neighbourhood locals called Greenland and did a shop, and then I went home and cooked myself an omelette with bacon, tomatoes and peppers on top. I didn't have any beer, so I had it with milk, thinking if my friends could see me now. And Duruta.

Afterwards I flung myself on the sofa to think and was snoozing by the time the telephone rang. It was Turið, she was hugely excited to tell me that she'd be coming home to the Faroes with her mum on Friday, and did I have her room ready for her? I told her that everything was prepared and cautiously asked where her mum would be staying? Turið wasn't really sure, but guessed it would be at Katrin and Karl's until they got their terraced house in Sodnhústún back on July 1st. She was in high spirits and also told me that Mum had insisted that Turið should live with Dad, so that the two of us could get to know each other better. I thought that may be true, but it could also be a means to forestall more panties in the bathroom.

I'd barely hung up when Karl phoned.

'Bergur told me about the conversation you two had with that Hans Petur Mørkøre. We've sent a request for information to Denmark to find out what happened to the Weihe family, and they've promised us an answer as soon as possible. There isn't much more we can do for now. We've questioned half of Klaksvík about the incident in Fagralíð, but nobody seems to have seen Ísak Joensen after he left his room at Sjómansheimi. The same is true for Áki Hansen and your car. We've come up empty-handed there too.'

'How about Látursgjógv, have you been in to check it out?'

'No, the sea is so choppy that those with local knowledge say it can't be done. One of these days we'll surely get at it, though.'

'One more thing, Karl. How come Katrin was so nice to me last night? For over six months I haven't dared approach your place. I mean, I haven't even spoken to you. I knew that the two of us would probably work things out sooner or later, but this overnight transformation in Katrin makes me smell a rat.'

'Oh nonsense. It's as I said last night, she likes you and then there's no reason to carry on holding a grudge about something for months on end.'

'Maybe,' I said, unconvinced.

Karl concluded by saying that although Bergur didn't want me any further tangled up in this matter, he'd make sure I heard from them when they got an update from Denmark.

I headed to the corridor and pulled the vacuum cleaner from the cupboard. The house was as filthy as a shag's nest, and I had to try and tidy up before my only daughter came home.

43

At Miðlahúsið they weren't pleased. That is, the editor wasn't pleased. As soon as he laid eyes on me he stormed out of his office, grabbed me by the arm, pulled me inside and shut the door.

'Where the fuck have you been hiding? I've called you more times than I can count.' His voice shook in sheer indignation.

I pulled my mobile from my pocket and noted that the sound was off. I could also see that I had 22 missed calls, and when I skimmed the list only Karl and my daughter had tried to catch me on this number. And then the editor, twenty times.

'Why've you been ringing me like that? We agreed that I wouldn't come in to work for two weeks. I've been digging out information about the deaths on the coast.'

'Are more people dead?' I'd caught the editor's attention.

'In addition to the guy in Fagralíð and the arm under Beinis-vørð, I've found another two.'

The editor was gobsmacked. When he found his voice again he nearly yelled: 'Bloody fucking hell Hannis, it'll be the story of the year! Have you written it?'

'No, because it's not finished yet, and I've promised Karl to wait.'

'I didn't think you and Karl were on speaking terms any more.'

'We're good now.'

'But you have a responsibility towards *Blaðið*. You work here.'

'Not these two weeks. Remember, you got Kim Hentze to sub for me.'

'You think so, do you? That's why I've been ringing you constantly, we need you. Kim bailed. I showed up the first day early in the morning, but no Kim. Then I called him, but no, he'd put his back out. Next day the same song, then it was a dentist's appointment that prevented him from coming into work. So I threw in the towel and left him in peace with his airport.'

'I can't return to work yet. Maybe in a couple of days. We'll see.'

The editor looked at me, shrugged and said, 'Ok, then we'll just write the story.'

'What story?'

'The one about all the skeletons.'

'What skeletons?'

The editor glared at me for a long time. 'You're a bloody bastard, you are, just get your arse back to work in two days max.'

Back outside on the Vágsbotnur waterfront, I asked myself why on earth I'd walked into Miðlahúsið in the first place. Force of habit was all I could conclude. I also started pondering where I should go to get dinner. I briefly considered calling Judith, but now Turið had told me that she and her mum would be back any day, I should probably lie low on that front. I was standing next to the car in Skálatrøð when my eye happened to catch the Irish Pub sign. That establishment had a menu with real steak and a glass of wine to go with it. Or a strong beer.

Weighing my options of wine or beer with dinner, I walked into the pub.

44

When I got to the hospital, there were only fifteen minutes left of the visiting hours, and the sun was well and truly in the west. There was almost a crowd down in the foyer, and the lift up to the ward where Edmund was currently lodged was near capacity. From the nurses' office his second cousin once removed waved with a smile when she spotted me.

Down at The Irish Pub, where I'd ordered their rib-eye steak with chips and two large glasses of Guinness, I'd been tempted to buy a beer for Edmund. But I knew that they weren't allowed to sell beer to go, so it was too much of a hassle.

When I entered the room, Edmund shouted, as I'd expected: 'Good man, I assume ye brought me a brew.'

And I replied, as he'd surely anticipated: 'Sorry, no, I couldn't do that my friend.'

'Couldn't!' said Edmund in a sharp tone. 'And they call themselves men. Can't even get their hands on a bottle of beer.'

The door opened and the cousin poked her head in to announce that visiting hours would be over in five minutes.

'Never mind that,' Edmund said. 'I've got the room to myself, and we're not disturbing anyone. The remark about the beer was only in jest. I haven't touched a drop in a week, so I spend part of my time here daydreaming about beer, wine and whisky. A real Macallan 50% wouldn't go amiss, with just a single drop of water in.' He closed his eyes and sighed: 'Mmmm.'

'How are you holding up?' I asked.

'Don't get me started! There are so many doctors poking and prodding me, and they can't agree on what's the matter. I'd swear it's only a bloody kidney stone that's become infected.

197

They've the fever under control at least. As ye can see: no drip.' Edmund demonstrated his arms freed from the tubes. Though the stand with the drip was still next to the bed.

'Well, then you'll be back home in a few days and we can have a cracking meal together paired with a choice beverage.'

'Sounds like heaven,' Edmund laughed and his glasses twinkled. 'But how goes it, have ye found anything out about *death on the shore?*' The latter was said in a tone of foreboding.

'I think so, but not enough yet,' and then I told Edmund the whole story. That they'd found the bloke who'd been shooting at me with his throat slit in a tunnel up north. How I'd been assaulted south in Trongisvágur and had met one of his many kinfolk there, and so on, right up to today when Bergur Mjóvanes and I grilled Hans Petur Mørkøre.

'Bloody hell,' Edmund muttered after all that, 'If I wasn't thirsty before, that story of yers certainly made me hanker for a drink.' He chuckled to himself.

'Ye said that the girl who was pierced by nails in the cave in Klaksvík was called Weihe?'

'Correct, her father was a grocer and they fled to Denmark shortly after it happened.'

'That Danish doctor who sees me the most, her name is Weihe too. Karen Weihe.'

'I thought her name was Vejen, Karen Vejen.'

'No, she...'

Just then the door opened and in came the Danish doctor. When she saw me she smiled, but said nothing. Her face was classically beautiful with grey eyes, straight nose and high cheekbones. Her lips were full and chin a little pointed. Thick blonde hair framed the whole.

'Ye won't be dying this year,' Edmund quipped.

'Pardon me?' she said in Danish.

'Perhaps ye've been yawning a lot lately?' he carried on, tongue-in-cheek.

'I'm afraid I don't follow.' She looked from Edmund over at me and back to Edmund.

'People usually say that when someone's talking about ye, ye start yawning.'

'Ah, I see,' she flashed a broad smile that revealed a row of pearly white teeth. I gathered that she understood Faroese.

'And what have you two been saying about me?'

'Oh, it was just that Hannis had garbled yer name to Karen Vejen, not Weihe.'

'Well, it's perhaps not that easy to hear the difference,' she laughed. 'And now it's time for your drip again, Mr. West.'

'I thought I was rid of it,' Edmund grumbled.

'It's only for tonight, I can guarantee you that.'

She inserted a needle into the crook of his left arm and secured it with a white plaster. Her fingers worked quickly, and were long and comely with sheer nail varnish on the short nails. Then she attached a translucent tube to the needle, swapped the IV bottle for one she was carrying in the pocket of her scrubs, and then fastened the tube to that. Slowly the drops started to trickle down through the tube and into Edmund's arm.

Just then my phone rang, and I answered, even though using mobiles wasn't allowed at the hospital. I didn't think it could do much harm here in Edmund's room.

'It's Karl. Where are you?'

'I'm at the hospital visiting Edmund,' I replied and glanced over at Karen Weihe, who was stroking Edmund's brow with a smile.

'We got a reply from Denmark, and it's a bombshell. Weihe's daughter, the one who allegedly died in Klaksvík in 1955, isn't dead. She was merely badly injured, but at Rigshospitalet in Copenhagen they got her back on her feet. Physically there was nothing wrong with her, but her psyche was fractured. The incident damaged her so much that you could never be sure what she was thinking. Her mind was sharp as a tack and she became a doctor, but was highly volatile and fell out with the Medical Association. The upshot was that they kicked her out, but she's still worked as a medic in various places in the Nordic region. She can be very charming, but she's two-faced, and you never know which personality is holding the reins. Is it the brilliant doctor, or is it the half-crazed one.'

The fair-haired woman approached.

'What's this woman's name?'

'Her name is Karen Weihe,' Karl said. In that split-second the doctor cut off the call on my mobile and showed me a scalpel she was holding in her right hand.

DARK MEMORY

Fallen
Without the fowling net.

45

Karen Weihe pressed the scalpel against my throat, and smiled. With her left hand she slipped my mobile into her pocket. I still found her beautiful, and she was so close that I caught a hint of perfume.

'You're coming with me now, quietly, over to the door.'

'You speak Faroese?'

'Of course I speak Faroese. I was born here and spent my first years in Klaksvík. That I've lived in Denmark since is a different story.'

I could feel the sharp blade under my chin and knew that the slightest movement of the hand holding the scalpel would leave me bleeding out like a slaughtered lamb. I looked over at Edmund who was lying with his eyes half-closed.

'He's slipping away and won't be waking up again. The bag contains a potent sedative and once he's had enough of that there'll be no return. If they perform an autopsy, they'll probably conclude it was cardiac arrest. The body breaks down the sedative in only a few hours, after which it's untraceable.'

Karin Weihe ordered me to place my hands behind my back, and I could feel her winding something around my wrists. Probably some form of tape. In that instant I could perhaps have put up a fight, but the scalpel never veered from my neck, so I thought it too risky.

Then she told me to open the door and go into the corridor. I had to do it behind my back, but managed to push the handle down and pull the door open. The corridor was deserted. So was the nurses' office.

'You can forget all about anyone coming to your rescue. I made sure that power was cut to the lifts and automatic doors, and I've locked all the doors to the staircase. No-one will be going anywhere for quite a while.'

She walked behind me holding the scalpel under my jaw and with her left hand on my shoulder. When we reached the door to the stairs, I stopped.

'Carry on, this one isn't locked.'

I opened in the same clumsy manner as before and we stepped onto the landing.

'We're going up,' Karin Weihe said. 'But don't you get any ideas, we'll take it sideways, nice and slow.'

As we sidled upwards, one step after the other, there was a pounding on doors and yelling in the distance, but we were the only ones on the staircase.

When we got to the top, I was again ordered to open a door, and obeyed. Evening light was slanting in the windows, and I could see that we'd reached a sizeable builders' workshop. Pots of paint lined shelves, one wall was covered in tool racks, and under the windows to one side stood a lathe with clamps.

I was commanded over to a chair with armrests, and a split second later the scalpel had cut off the ties on my wrists.

'Sit down and place your hands on the armrests.' The scalpel was back below my chin. With the left hand she now secured my wrists to the chair using gaffer tape. My ankles were tied together in the same way, but the scalpel was no longer on my jugular.

Through the windows on one side I could see across a picket fence towards Sandagerð beach and the suburb, Argir, and to the other side I could make out the oil terminal and the salt store. We were in a little black extension on the hospital rooftop. Not exactly a place where you would expect footfall, at least not in the evening.

Karin Weihe pulled up a chair and gazed at me, smiling. Chills ran down my spine when she said: 'Well then, whatever shall we do with you now?'

46

Karin Weihe flashed a smile, but I thought I detected madness in her eyes. Or maybe it was just because I knew it was there.

She came so close I could feel a gentle waft of perfume as she stroked my cheek with her fingertips.

'Oh darling, you look quite sweet to me. Why did you get yourself caught up in all this?' The voice had a flirtatious erotic lilt.

'I'm a journalist, it's hardly surprising that I'd want to look into a dead body found shackled on the shore.'

'I suppose you're right. It wasn't meant to turn out like this either, that was never the plan. That bloody idiot, Áki, ruined everything.'

'So you knew Áki Hansen?' I asked.

'It was me who got him to come home. Promised him golden days if he'd help me with something.'

'This help consisted in killing Ísak Joensen, I presume.'

'It did,' the doctor said with a stone-cold expression. 'He well and truly deserved it, but it was never meant to be done in plain sight. But Áki was so astoundingly stupid and lazy that he couldn't be bothered to go any further than the shore in Fagralíð.' She gazed pensively at the scalpel.

'Why shouldn't the murder be public?' I hastened to ask, before she got any ideas.

'Ísak Joensen was meant to die like the others before him. Knowing that death was inescapable, that there was nothing he could do to prevent it.'

'Why did they have to die like that?'

She looked me in the eye and said, 'Do you know what they did to me? Have you any idea of the suffering they put me through?' Her eyes burned as she unbuttoned the top of her scrubs and pulled it down. Several bright white scars were revealed on her chest.

'And all this is nothing. My abdomen and pelvis were riddled with thick nails, and I was just a little girl. I lived, but only after they'd had to cut so much out of me that I could never have children.'

'I know that what these guys did is unforgiveable, but why did they have to be killed in that way?'

She glared at me for a moment, 'You keep referring to them as men, but two women were a part of this, and they were probably the worst. So one of them was killed as the first.'

'You were a child, you can't have played much of a role in that.'

'Of course not. But I had a father whose life was ruined because of those bastards in Klaksvík. And by that I don't just mean the lunatics in The Niners, but the villagers in general. They smashed the windows both at the shop and in our home several times, my brothers were stoned and beaten on a regular basis and my parents refused to let me out of their sight, because they were terrified someone would hurt me. Until one afternoon I did manage to sneak out, and you know what came of that.'

She twirled and took a couple of dance steps, softly singing the romantic waltz, 'Kom og dansa, hjartans kæri skattur mín...' Suddenly she went quiet and turned back towards me.

'Even though Father was a wreck in many ways, he had sufficient strength and money to take revenge. My brothers were half-grown, and it was them who killed that first woman. Marianna I think she was called. When Father found out he was furious, and it also hastened my parents' decision to leave the country. On top of the fact that I was hospitalised in Copenhagen. But my brothers' deed gave my father an idea. How he managed, I don't know, but he got in touch with professionals willing to take on the task of murdering four people in Klaksvík in a particular way.'

She looked me straight in the eye, 'I surmise you know the way.'

I nodded.

'Father insisted in his instructions that these people weren't just to be killed, but that they should suffer for as long as possible, know that death was inevitable. And that they should be shackled. These men then travelled to the Faroes and three of the people who'd taken me captive were found and left in caves to meet their maker. The fourth was Ísak Joensen, he'd fled the country so they couldn't track him down.'

A motor started up and a screech of cables could be heard. The lifts were clearly back up and running.

Karin Weihe grinned, 'Ah, they managed to locate the fault. I should probably show my face, so they won't miss me down on the ward. Don't be sad, I won't be long.'

Then she left.

47

When she'd left I tried to tear myself free, but it was no use. You can't just rip gaffer tape. So I started hopping with the chair towards the door to the staircase. That went quite well. Once I made it over I pushed on the handle. It didn't budge, she'd wedged it with something.

What to do now? And what about Edmund? He'd die if nobody pulled out that drip. Maybe it was already too late? I pushed that thought away and tried to focus on freeing myself.

Wasn't there anything sharp lying around, so I could slit the gaffer tape? No matter how hard I looked, nothing seemed of use. At least nothing I could get my wrists anywhere in the vicinity of. On the wall with the tools there were several wood chisels, and they were usually sharp. The problem was that there was a wooden workbench up against the wall.

The chair and I hopped over to the table. It looked sturdy and heavy. It would be hard to shift it even an inch. And to get at the tools I'd have to move it roughly a metre. But how?

Between the workbench and the wall there was a long ridged radiator. It was a little longer than the table, and when I placed the back of my chair up against the end of the table, I managed to brace my feet against the radiator's ridges.

Inch by inch I nudged the workbench along. It was a struggle and I was drenched in sweat, but in the end I was sitting right below several wood chisels on the wall. They were mounted in racks and the blades were sticking out at the bottom. The blade edges were level with my shoulders, and I planned to use one shoulder to lift a wood chisel out of the rack, so it would drop to the floor. I should be able to get my wrists to it from there.

My first attempts to push a chisel from its mount failed. For one, I was too cautious. I knew how sharp they could be. But eventually I lifted my shoulder with sufficient force, and a slender one toppled out of its mount, somersaulted and dug itself into a cross beam under the workbench top.

As if on cue, the door opened and Karin Weihe came in. Luckily, I was positioned between her and the cross beam with the chisel, so hopefully she wouldn't spot it.

'Well, well', she laughed. 'I clearly returned in the nick of time.' She approached me with the scalpel in her right hand.

'Let me see.' She checked both my wrists with her left hand and said, 'It doesn't appear you've achieved much yet. If you're good, you'll live. At least for a while longer.' And then she burst into a crazed cackle, which ended just as abruptly as it started.

'I was lucky that I went downstairs,' she said in an utterly normal tone. 'A couple of your friends were visiting. Karl Olsen and Bergur Mjóvanes from the Criminal Investigation Department. They wanted to know where you were. I said that I'd spoken to you, but that you'd left shortly after visiting hours. Then they wanted to talk to Edmund West, but he happened to be sleeping,' she said with a grin and looked straight into my eyes. Then she winked, as if the two of us shared a secret.

48

I noticed that part of the wood chisel was at the height of my right wrist. The side wasn't razor sharp, not like the cutting edge, but maybe sharp enough to file through the gaffer tape.

I shuffled the chair a little closer to the table, and Karin Weihe didn't seem to notice. She was staring into space instead, and said: 'It's curious really, if you think about it, that the Danish Medical Association, which had such a big share of responsibility for the Klaksvík Revolt, was also partly responsible for Ísak Joensen getting his punishment. They gave me a warning for not taking sufficiently good care of a drug addict in Vestre Fængsel Prison. Said that he died because of my mistake. It was no mistake. The bastard was such a wretch anyway that he was better off departing this earth. I saw no reason to prevent it.'

With that she held my gaze to check if I agreed with what she was saying. The way things stood, I had no appetite to contradict her and so I nodded in confirmation. She carried on: 'Naturally, I refused to accept the warning, I didn't believe I'd done anything wrong, but rather the only right thing. The upshot was that I was barred from the Medical Association and so couldn't practise medicine in Denmark. Instead I've been working in both Sweden and Norway for years, and now for the last few months here in the Faroes.'

She walked over to a window and looked out, 'It was pure chance that I spotted Ísak Joensen. Father had so often shown me photos of this man and told me that, if possible, I should make sure he got his due. I was at the airport picking up a Danish locum when the flight from Iceland landed, and who came strolling out as if he'd never committed a sin? Ísak Joensen. An older man, but still easy to recognise. I swear that my heart stopped for several minutes, and I don't know how I got the locum into the car and drove to Tórshavn, but I managed.'

She turned around. 'I knew instantly this was my chance to eliminate that monster. First I considered doing it myself, and I should have!' she declared passionately. 'What a fool I was to contact Áki Hansen. I'd met him when I was working at Vestre Fængsel Prison, and I knew he could be made to do no matter what for money. That he would simply do *no matter what*, instead of as instructed, that I didn't know. And now I'm paying for it.' She grinned at me. 'And so are you and several others. Had Áki Hansen done as he was told, then nobody, except for that old devil from Klaksvík, would have needed to die.'

'Why did he try to kill me?' I asked, pressing the gaffer tape against the wood chisel.

'He was acting entirely on his own initiative there. I'd told him to keep an eye on you, and when you went traipsing around Klaksvík asking if anyone would sail you out to that gorge in Kunoy Island, he had an idea. I'd given him such an earful for Ísak Joensen that now he wanted to finish you off to get back into my good books. More fool him. The rest you know. Slitting his throat was the only thing for it.'

There was no doubt. Karin Weihe was absolutely convinced that she was doing what had to be done. She was some kind of psychopath. Had become one because of her ordeal. One trait that's characteristic of psychopaths is that they can always come up with arguments justifying that they are doing the right thing. No matter how despicable it may be.

'You never answered the question as to why these people had to be killed out of sight,' I said, while trying to cut into the tape around my wrist. 'That they should just disappear.'

'That's what father wanted. He said that these deeds of darkness shouldn't become public gossip. That's why he was adamant that they should die far from where people might go. And that they should suffer and be tortured until their dying breath.'

213

This last declaration she proclaimed as if she was reading the Bible. I also had a vague recollection that old Weihe had been a devout man. I filed away warily with my wrists against the wood chisel, as I tried to keep the conversation going.

'Was it you who went to Suðuroy to get the bag of bones?'

'I heard what Edmund shouted after you when we came on our rounds, and I was perhaps the only person in this country who could put two and two together. I was chilled to the marrow. I knew that one of the perpetrators had been concealed in a cave under Beinisvørð and I knew of the rockslide. It wasn't likely that an unrelated shackled arm had been found on the island. In order to keep my promise to Father that the deeds of darkness should be concealed, I went south.'

'But how did you know where to look?'

'Oh, I went to the care home and spoke to the old policeman. I'm a doctor after all, and he was delighted that I showed him such interest. In exchange, he told me about those bones a relative in Tórshavn had phoned about.'

Something else came to mind: 'The woman who was shoved out of the way at the policeman's house said it was a man who came charging out of the door.'

'I brought along a man's coat and a hat and put them on before entering the house.'

'What about the footprint? It was a size 42 according to the police.'

'I've got big feet,' said the doctor and showed me one of her shoes. It was a short black boot and for a woman, it was big.

'What did you do with the canvas bag the arm was in?'

'I dumped it overboard from *Smyril* on my way north.'

That was what I thought, and now the tape was beginning to tear.

'And it was also you who trashed my place?'

'Yes, I don't know what came over me. I knew that you'd gone back to Suðuroy. I saw you and that skinny hag over in SMS. The one who works at the care home Lágargarður. Later, a fat couple arrived. I followed you down to the harbour, and once you'd left with *Smyril*, I went out to your place. I was angry and lost control, and then...' Her look was almost apologetic. But the scalpel at the ready never dipped.

'But why are you trying to kill me and Edmund?'

'It certainly wasn't my initial plan, but you're like snares around my feet. The other evening, when I'd made sure that the nurses were busy elsewhere, you were there. Edmund West is sick and, from my perspective, he knows too much. So it's quite straightforward really.'

Her conclusion was simple: 'A sick creature, especially one that's a pest, needs to be put down.'

She walked right up to me and looked me in the eye. 'You, I hadn't intended to do any more about. Had I wanted to, I could've done it down south, but now you've come too close. There's little else to do other than eliminate you.'

'The detectives who were here also know most of the details. You can't kill them too,' I attempted.

'Well, we shall see about that. Let's deal with one nuisance at a time.' Her eyes were ablaze with madness, and she raised the scalpel.

That was when my right hand came free. I grabbed the shaft of the wood chisel, pulled it loose and flung it at Karin Weihe's foot.

A spray of blood shot up, she screamed and swung at me with the scalpel. She was aiming for my throat, but she was unsteady on her feet now and hit my upper arm instead. The blade sliced straight to the bone. She tumbled backwards in the same movement, while her foot was still nailed to the floor with the wood chisel.

In one breath I managed to loosen the tape around my other wrist and ankles and scuttled stiff-legged across the room. I got the door open, and with my left hand attempting to staunch the bleeding from my right arm, I bolted down the stairs.

49

Blood was seeping between my fingers, and I could feel the arm weakening; I could hardly use it. The scalpel had cut clean through ligaments and muscles, but I'd escaped alive, for now. I'd made it to the first staircase landing when it occurred to me that I should perhaps have tried to tackle the mad doctor. The hitch was just that she had a scalpel, and I couldn't use my right arm. Better to run for help.

I got the door open and entered the corridor. The ceiling lights were on, but it seemed strangely deserted here. As if the ward was not in use. It was dark in the nurses' office, and there wasn't a sound on the whole floor. I poked my head into a room here and there, but they were empty, sterile and clinical. It was almost as if the ward had been refurbished and now stood shiny and empty.

I rushed to the nurses' office and picked up the phone. Nothing. I left it and headed to the lifts, but that area was deserted too. I had to get away from here. This was a death trap.

That was when I heard the sound of the door to the staircase, and I raced into the office and under a table.

I heard the door open, and someone came limping and swearing down the corridor.

'You fucking arsehole, you won't get away from me, no matter how you try to sneak off and hide. You're bleeding, all I have to do is follow your trail. I'll make sure you wind up in the torture chamber of the damned.'

Shortly after she was standing right outside the office, breathing heavily. I could hear her scraping against the glass pane, no doubt trying to peer into the half-darkness. Then she carried on down the corridor. I heard her enter one of the rooms, was planning to get up and race to the staircase when I heard her return like a limping devil right outside. I stayed put.

For a heartbeat it was completely quiet. She was listening. Then she went back to panting and hobbling along the corridor, talking to herself: 'Wonder if the bastard's left this floor? There's blood everywhere,' she muttered. 'Can't tell his from mine.'

The door to the staircase opened and shut.

A deadly silence followed, but I was acutely aware that this was no place to stay, so I headed for the same door the crazed doctor had gone through.

Warily, I pressed the handle down and opened the door a crack. I couldn't see anyone, and couldn't hear anything either. I slipped quietly outside and was planning to take the stairs down when I spotted Karin Weihe, standing with the scalpel at the ready only a few steps below.

'I'll castrate you,' she screamed and swung the scalpel. There was a blood trail along the stairs where she'd dragged her foot, and I could see it oozing from her shoe.

My only option was to retreat up the stairs and back into the workshop. Safely inside, I looked to see if there was anything I could shove under the door handle. But no, not with only one functioning arm. Couldn't see anything I could use as defence against a scalpel either, not with my left hand.

The door to the roof wasn't locked, so I went out and rounded the corner of the black extension to its windowless side. The weather was stunning and the setting sun gilded both sea and land. Didn't do me much good, though. The railing around the roof was quite high, but facing the Álaker boatyard it had been removed between two steel posts. I went over and found a scaffolding platform suspended one floor below.

An idea struck me and I seized it, thinking it was my only way out. I loosened the grip around my right overarm and the bleeding started again. The arm was nearly dead, but I shook it the little I could as I moved back towards the extension. Then I applied pressure again and took cover.

As I rounded the corner, I heard the door open, followed by Karin Weihe's limping gait along the roof, then she came into sight. Her eyes were fixed on the blood trace and she followed it over towards the hole in the railings. Me she couldn't see.

Once there she leaned out over the edge to look where I'd gone. In the meantime, I'd snuck up close enough to give her a push that sent her flailing over the edge. Half a breath later there was a thump from below.

I didn't look down, didn't think it necessary. Instead I rushed inside and down the stairs. I knew time was running out for Edmund.

50

When I came to, Karl was sitting by my bedside. He handed me a glass of water and said:

'Good job they were willing to take you in here at the hospital. One dead consultant, a power cut, and then they find you unconscious half under Edmund West's bed hugging his IV stand.'

'How's Edmund?' I croaked, barely audible.

'Edmund's fit as a fiddle. You saved him when you pulled the IV from his arm. What's more, the kidney stone that was making him ill came out while he was sleeping. That sedative the doctor pumped into him made his body relax, so the stone slipped out with the urine. He did wet the bed all right, but rather that than staying in here. Edmund was discharged yesterday.'

'Yesterday? How long have I been out?'

'Since the night before last. You were sedated and operated on immediately. You'd lost a lot of blood and had to have a transfusion. The doctor who took care of you says that the arm will probably be fine, but that it'll take its time.'

'So it's Friday,' I said with a vague recollection that something was meant to be happening that day.

'It's Friday evening. It's past dinnertime.'

I glanced to the right where my arm lay in a splint wrapped in bandages. I could move my fingers when I tried, though, so it could be worse.

'What about Karin Weihe?' I asked, reliving the image of her flailing into the void.

'There was nothing that could be done. She died on impact.'

'A tragic fate,' I said.

'I agree with you there, but it still didn't warrant her and her family murdering people left, right and centre. In some respect it was a terrible accident. As far as I've understood, the Niners never intended to harm the girl.'

'So what would you call getting shackled in a cave as a little girl?' Karl didn't reply, and I continued: 'What happened in that cave damaged her. Something happened in her head. Getting pierced by four-inch nails isn't exactly fun.'

'No, it's not,' Karl said. 'Even so, it wasn't necessary to murder those people in such a sickeningly gruesome manner.'

'You're supposed to say that, you're an officer of the law. And your daughters are grown too. But if anyone did to Turið what those people did to the girl Karin, I wouldn't let them get away with it unscathed.'

'You mentioned Turið,' Karl smiled. 'She's sitting in the waiting room with Duruta. They arrived on the plane this morning. Should I go and get them?'

I nodded, finally remembering what was meant to be happening on Friday.

Moments later Turið came running into the room shouting, 'Daddy!' and she came over and hugged me. I thought of the poet's words, 'More beautiful than the bay of Tórshavn is the word father,' and I agreed. That was when I caught sight of Duruta who was standing in the doorway with a neat bump. She must be seven months along. She was smiling too, but still looked a little nervous. She came over to me and took my left hand and gave it a squeeze.

While Turið told me about everything she'd experienced in Copenhagen and everything she had planned now that they were moving back home again, I lay there looking up at Duruta.

To me she looked more stunning than ever. The straight brown hair and the lively dark eyes.

Karl poked his head inside and asked if Turið didn't want to join him for a trip down to the kiosk, so that her parents could have a moment to themselves. Turið was happy to oblige, but when the door to the corridor closed, we didn't know what to say. We'd grown shy around each other.

Duruta was the one to break the silence. 'You know, that thing I told you, about finding another man when I moved to Denmark.'

I nodded.

'I only said it because I was so furious with you. Wanted you to feel what it was like. I haven't slept with anyone but you.' Duruta gazed into my eyes, serious.

'Does that mean...' I said in a hoarse voice.

Duruta nodded with a smile.

JÓGVAN ISAKSEN

Walpurgis Tide

(translated by John Keithsson)

Two British environmental activists are discovered dead amongst the whale corpses after a whale-kill in Tórshavn. The detective Hannis Martinsson is asked to investigate by a representative of the organisation Guardians of the Sea – who shortly afterwards is killed when his private plane crashes. Suspicion falls on Faroese hunters, angry at persistent interference in their traditional whale hunt; but the investigation leads Martinsson to a much larger group of international vested interests, and the discovery of a plot which could devastate the whole country.

ISBN 9781909408241
UK £13.95
(Paperback, 282 pages)

JØRGEN-FRANZ JACOBSEN

Barbara

(translated by George Johnston)

Barbara, originally written in Danish, was the only novel by the Faroese author Jørgen-Franz Jacobsen (1900-1938), and yet it quickly achieved international best-seller status and is still one of the best-loved twentieth-century classics in Danish and Faroese literature. On the face of it, *Barbara* is a straightforward historical novel in the mode of many a so-called 'romance'. It contains a story of passion in an exotic setting with overtones of semi-piracy; there is a powerful erotic element, an outsider who breaks up a marriage, and a built-in inevitability resulting from Barbara's own psychological make-up. She stands as one of the most complex female characters in modern Scandinavian literature: beautiful, passionate, innocent, devoted, amoral and uncomprehending of her own tragedy. Jørgen-Franz Jacobsen portrays her with a fascinated devotion.

ISBN 9781909408074
UK £13.95
(Paperback, 306 pages)

JAN KJÆRSTAD

Berge

(translated by Janet Garton)

One August day in 2008 the Norwegian Labour Party's most colourful MP, Arve Storefjeld, is discovered in a remote cabin in the country, together with four of his family and friends, all with their throats slit. This unprecedented crime in the peaceful backwater of Norway sends shudders through the national psyche, as the search for the perpetrators begins and people have to adjust to the terrifying thought: it can happen here too. The rapidly unfolding events are narrated from the standpoints of three observers who in different ways become drawn in to the investigation: Ine Wang, a young journalist who has just finished a biography of Storefjeld and realises that the tragedy has presented her with an irresistible scoop; Peter Malm, a judge whose ideal of a quiet contemplative life away from public scrutiny is turned upside-down by his unwilling involvement in the case; and Nicolai Berge, a former boyfriend of one of the victims, who emerges as the main suspect and a focus for the public demand for catharsis. Published six years after the trauma of 22 July 2011, when 77 Norwegians were killed in a one-man assault on the government offices in Oslo and a Young Labour camp on the island of Utøya, Jan Kjærstad's novel explores the vulnerabilities of modern life and the terrifying unpredictability of acts of terror.

ISBN 9781909408531
UK £14.95
(Paperback, 400 pages)

www.ingramcontent.com/pod-product-compliance
Ingram Content Group UK Ltd.
Pitfield, Milton Keynes, MK11 3LW, UK
UKHW030211070125
453255UK00009B/149